SHEEP

By

G. Novitsky

ISBN: 1-4107-9928-X (e-book)
ISBN: 1-4107-9929-8 (Paperback)

This book is printed on acid free paper.

1stBooks — rev. 09/15/03

Dedication

For

Richard and Danielle

*Regardless of how unfair or displeasing
something life hands you may seem, remember,
there is always a deeper meaning for it.
The love and blessings that surround you
will always outweigh the disappointments.
Be strong and embrace the positives.*

Chapter One
"Dr. Bleckard"

March 2003

Dr. Albert Bleckard walked down the aisle toward the stage to accept his award for scientific accomplishments. Dr. Bleckard, a forty-one year old scientist has been an esteemed member of the scientology division in New England for many years. He moved here to The States at a young age to further his education.

He has been studying human behavior and all types of animals and organisms since he was twelve years old. That made him quite different from the other children his age. Another one of his passions was hypnotism. He became a hypnotist at the age of seventeen.

The crowd cheered as he made his way to the podium. Dr. Bleckard was very well known, adored, and respected in the scientific community. This community may seem boring to many others, but I assure you that Dr. Bleckard will shock the hell out of you with some of his experiments.

With his English accent, Dr. Bleckard opened his speech. He complimented the audience on their choice of clothing and then joked about the looks on their faces. The crowd laughed.

"I cannot thank you enough for your overly warm welcome and flattering admiration of my work. I don't want to bore you like so many others in the field do. I will keep it short and sweet. I know that many of you enjoyed some of my outcomes, not to mention my mishaps. Let's not even bring up the three-alarm blaze outside of London last year or my minor portion of assistance on an undercover investigation." Bert commented, as his good friend in the crowd put his head down and whispered to the man next to him that he couldn't believe he brought that up.

I would just like to announce that what I believe is in its final stages in my laboratory will shock and amaze the entire world. If all goes according to plan I should be presenting it in the next two to three months." Dr. Bleckard said his thank you and headed off back stage. The audience was anxious to see what the big presentation was going to be. There was a roar over the crowd.

He loved to leave the audience in suspense and he usually did. The laboratory he spoke of was located in a Connecticut farmland. He had it specially built close to twenty-five years ago for his upcoming projects. Dr. Bleckard, a tall thin man with a beard and mustache, went by the name of Albert; his closest friends referred to him as Bert.

Bert grew up outside of London with his father, mother and older brother up until the age of eleven when he lost his mother. She died of a disease known as Lupus. The disease was not very well known around the time she was diagnosed with it. All Bert knew about it at the time was, his mother's healthy cells were fighting against themselves causing many problems in her organs.

2

March 1974

After his mother's death, Bert and his brother became very depressed. His brother packed up and headed to The States at the age of seventeen. Bert started spending all of his free time at the lab in school. He worked on some of his own projects and kept his head in his books just so he wouldn't have to face the world outside. He wanted to learn more about the disease that was said to take the life of his mother. That's when he began his journey into medicine and the human body.

He also began questioning religion and whether or not God existed. Aside from his interest in Science, he also made time to explore other areas of religion and creation. He was drawn to the darker side of religion, which was more mysterious to him.

The other kids in school would notice that Bert was in his own world and they would give him a hard time once in a while. One day, a week after he turned twelve years old, some of the kids were giving him a hard time in an atrium type yard between a couple of the school buildings. One of the boys started to go through his book-bag. The boy came across a bible. It wasn't a bible that most of us are used to. It was a satanic bible.

The boy picked it up and realized what it was. Quickly he threw it to the floor and spit on his hands to clean the devil off of them. The boy then cursed Bert. "What is wrong with you? Are you a bloody fool? You are not supposed to touch that stuff." The boy yelled. The boy's name was Scott. As Scott ran away, the other two boys gave Bert the beating of his life. The beating seemed to last for hours in Bert's mind. When it was finally over Bert gathered his things and headed to the boy's room to clean himself up.

That beating left a lasting impression on Bert. It increased his interest in the dark bible that the other kids were extremely against. Bert read the book from cover to cover and that made him even more curious about Satan and the dark religion.

Over the course of the next year he read several other books on the subject and he gained a large amount of knowledge about it. Bert also avoided those boys at all costs through the remainder of the school year.

Bert knew in his heart that all of the things he learned about Satanism and the dark religion were wrong, but that only fueled his interest.

February 1977

When he was old enough, in his teenage years he attended a satanic mass. He found out where they were held from some of his reading materials.

Bert was very nervous when he arrived at the church. He stood in front with a strange feeling in his stomach. He noticed other people going inside. They were all dressed in black, and they had cold stares on their faces.

Bert finally built up his nerve to go inside. He walked in slowly and took a seat near the door. There was evil sounding music playing as a tall frightening man in a black robe approached the altar. The man had a similar book to the one Bert used to bring to school. The book was tucked under the man's arm.

The man started to read from the book in a low scary voice. "Followers, I will lead you on your journey to find a true leader who will not fill your head with lies and deceit." The man said before he started the ceremony.

The mass lasted for about an hour and Bert made it through the whole thing. He didn't participate in the drinking of the lamb's blood or any of the other festivities that took place there.

Bert left with somewhat of an understanding of what it was all about and he didn't think it was the worst choice that someone could make for a life style. He felt it had some kind of direction.

Bert walked into his house later than he expected he would. His father was up waiting for him. "How many times do I have to tell you not to come strolling in here whenever you bloody well feel?" His father asked. Bert could tell that his father had been drinking again. "I'm sorry father." Is all Bert said and then headed to his room. His room was big enough for three kids. Bert and his father lived in a very large house. His father was extremely well off financially. The money in the family was handed down from generation to generation.

Bert's father had been drinking himself to sleep almost every night since the loss of his wife. This drove Bert and his father further and further apart. Bert understood his father's depression, but he also thought that his father should understand that he was experiencing equal depression from the same loss.

Bert realized that staying with his father was not beneficial to either one of them. He still loved his dad, but he started to think about his future and how his father's money would help him get a start in the world.

Over the next couple of years Bert continued with his interests in Satan and the human mind and body, but he also focused a great deal on his regular school studies. He looked into the route his brother took, he only hoped he wouldn't run into him in The States.

September 1979

With perfect grades and a couple hundred thousand dollars of his dad's money, at the age of seventeen Bert was able to set up residence and pay college tuition at one of the finest colleges in New England.

The college Dean was overly impressed with Bert's Academic performance. Bert received special attention from all of the professors and staff at the college. That made his experience there very comfortable and it allowed him free rein to perform experiments using the school Science lab.

Bert amazed the other students and professors with some of his experiments, his knowledge of science and how he knew his way around the laboratory. Some of the students told him that he would change the future of science and they joked calling him Dr. Frankenstein.

The college also offered many language classes as part of the curriculum. Bert decided to take advantage of the offer and he signed up for a course in Latin. He felt that Latin had a darkness to it and it wasn't a language that many of the other students were lining up to learn.

There was a strange young man in the Latin class named Pete. Bert took a liking to him immediately. Pete would sit in the back of the classroom before the professor came in and he would hypnotize some of the classmates. They all got a kick out of it.

Pete tried many times to hypnotize Bert but he was never successful. Pete said it had to do with Bert's overly strong mind. He would mostly hypnotize the girls in the class and have them act somewhat provocative towards the guys. The guys really appreciated it.

Pete was eventually thrown out of the school but before that he brought Bert to some shows involving hypnotists and he taught him most of his own tricks of the trade.

October 1980

After his first semester, Bert decided that he needed something a little more than his small house off campus. He started looking for something bigger where he could set up a lab of his own. After quite a long search for an appropriate location, his sights were set on a deserted farmland in Connecticut. It had the size he was looking for, plus it was a place that he could design and build from the ground up.

After he sold his house, Bert lived on campus and made trips on the weekends to his new investment. He met with several construction companies to find one to build his dream laboratory, and finally went with one, Morris Construction Inc.

The owner of the company was Carl Morris. Bert felt very comfortable with Carl, and that was important. Carl was a very hard worker but he was far from the brightest crayon in the box. Bert and Carl went over exactly how and where Bert wanted everything. It took months to get it perfect.

Carl thought that some of Bert's ideas were strange in the beginning, like garage doors leading into the house. Once Carl had it explained to him that Bert was planning on setting up a laboratory and that there was going to be a lot of equipment moved in, it all made sense.

Bert was still attending college in New England. Besides all of the attention that he was receiving from the Dean, the professors, and the staff, Bert realized that many of the college girls were paying special attention to him also. Although he was only eighteen, Bert didn't have a problem passing for twenty-one or twenty-two. No one ever questioned him to be younger than he said he was.

One girl named Stephanie tried very hard to get Bert to notice her. That wasn't very difficult. Stephanie was twenty-one years old, blonde and beautiful. Although Bert was not like an average guy who thinks about women twenty-four hours a day, he did have an interest in Stephanie.

Bert and Stephanie started eating their lunches together, and then dinners. Soon enough Bert started working on science projects with her. He felt that she could be a good partner for some of his experiments.

One night after working late together, they both felt like they needed to get out for a while. They went to a bar off campus. After a few drinks, they started laughing and telling each other about their lives and how they ended up going to school in New England.

Bert suddenly felt uncomfortable. "Something's wrong." He said. "What is it?" She asked. "I am starting to feel like my father used to look." Bert said. "What does that mean?" Stephanie asked. Bert then explained to Stephanie how his father became an alcoholic after his mother's death. "We don't have to drink anymore. We could go back to my dorm room and talk if you want." She suggested. "I have an even better idea." Bert said. "What would that be?" Stephanie asked. "How would you like to be the first to see the place I set up in Connecticut?" He asked. "That would be really nice, but do you feel like driving all that way?" She questioned. "Yes, I do." Bert replied.

They left a tip on the bar, got into Bert's car and headed to the house. During the ride Stephanie couldn't keep her hands off him. Bert was getting very turned on and he began to touch Stephanie in return.

When they finally arrived at Bert's place they were overcome with their attraction toward one another. Bert walked her through a couple of rooms as he groped her on the way to the bedroom.

She started to loosen up her jeans to give him a slight peak of her panties as she walked. She held on to one of his hands and gently caressed it over her curves. Bert became flustered. He couldn't make it to the bedroom. He made his way on to his knees and started to kiss her stomach and hips.

They decided enough was enough, as they tore each other's clothes off and made passionate love for close to two hours on the floor.

When that was all finished and they were able to locate all of their clothes, Bert showed Stephanie the rest of the house. She was very impressed. "You could use some nice curtains and wallpaper." Stephanie joked. "Maybe one day I will let you decorate." Bert said. They talked for a while, after a few hours, they both fell asleep.

Chapter Two
"The Maine Event"

February 1981

Monday morning Bert was back at his classes. He was going over some of the papers he had written for his English Literature class with his professor Dr. Arthur Hynes. Arthur was in his early thirties; he was a tall man with a beard and some gray in his hair. He has been married for over six years.

Dr. Hynes was very impressed by all of Bert's writings. Most of all, he was astonished at the one about Satanism. "I love what you have done with this one. It is extremely informative and it makes me feel as if I was with you when you experimented with the subject. How were you able to obtain so much information on a subject such as this?" Dr. Hynes asked.

"When I was younger something drew me towards studying the extremities of religions. I was a bit curious about this one aspect and once I began looking into it, my curiosity just grew from there. Of course that was a long while ago and I filled my curiosity, now I just write about it as I do with all of my studies." Bert said.

I didn't think that you were a worshiper. You seem to be well beyond that type of evilness. I do find your writing astonishing though. With your permission, I would like to have this manuscript published and made available in our campus library." Dr. Hynes requested.

"That sounds fine by me, and if there is any kind of financial gain from it, maybe we can donate it towards the library, or toward some kind of an outreach program that supports children who are unsure of where to direct their faith, or something like that." Bert suggested.

"You never cease to amaze me Albert. That is an honorable suggestion. I will let the publishing company know that they have something very special coming their way." Dr. Hynes said.

Dr. Hynes has been a professor at the college for close to five years. He was very outgoing and a man of his word. If he said Bert's story would be published, then Bert's story would be published.

Bert and Dr. Hynes spent a lot of their free time together discussing literature and other interests of theirs over the next few weeks. Dr. Hynes invited Bert to join him for a weekend in Maine to catch lobster. That was Dr. Hynes' passion. He enjoyed the sea, bringing back his favorite foods and getting away for a couple of days with the tranquility of the ocean.

Before they left for their trip, Bert decided to give Stephanie a call to let her know he was going to be away for the weekend. He had not seen her in a while. He wanted to see if there was anything special that he could bring her back from Maine.

"The damn answering machine again, Arty. That's the third time in the last three phone calls. Maybe she doesn't like me anymore. Hi Steph. It's me, Bert, leaving another message. I am going to Maine for the weekend. I hope we can get together when I return. Bye, bye." Bert said.

"Maybe she's bored with all of your love for science and constant studying. Girls like that need fun in their life also." Dr. Hynes said. "Maybe you're right. Maybe I'll plan something fun for me and her when we get back." Bert said.

When they got to the area, it was exactly how Dr. Hynes explained it, a small piece of paradise for a fisherman. "Before I show you my boat, I want you to see the cottage where we will be staying tonight. It's beautiful. It's well out of the way of the locals and no one really knows it's here." Dr. Hynes said, as they drove through some back roads with only trees around them.

They parked the car and walked down a slight hill. At the bottom was a small cottage that Dr. Hynes liked to call his home away from home.

"Make yourself comfortable. Have a drink." Dr Hynes said. "I don't mind if I do. Ahhh, Sprite. Now I'm at home. Hold my calls." Bert said with a child like grin on his face.

Dr. Hynes showed Bert around and told him how once every year or so he buys all of the supplies he needs to last him for his next one hundred trips to the cottage. He showed him where he stashes all of his canned foods, soda, beer, and snacks in the cellar.

"This is a mighty fine set up Arty. I really like what you have here." Bert said. "Thank you. Now it's about time to see the main reason we're here. Get it? Maine reason. That's just some state humor. Come on; let's go to the boat." Dr. Hynes said.

When they got to the boat, Bert was just as impressed as he was with the cottage. "It's not the greatest, but it's comfortable, and it gets the job done."

Dr. Hynes said. The boat was aged but it was rather large. It had a separate eating area and bathroom. There was also a small area where two people could sleep comfortably.

The guys took the boat out on the beautiful sea and caught some lobsters and shrimp. Bert was more entertained by just being out on the water than he was by all of the seafood. Bert had been a man of many talents and gifted with knowledge, but this was his first time on a boat, and he couldn't get enough of it.

He sat on the bow smiling. Dr. Hynes was pleased to make it such a wonderful experience for his favorite student. Before the ride was over, Bert made Dr. Hynes promise that he would take him out there again.

In the morning Bert asked Dr. Hynes to take him down to the village so he could pick something up for Stephanie. He found a charm necklace of a boat with a heart in it. He felt that would fit the occasion. He also bought a Captains hat for Dr. Hynes. Bert gave him the hat on the ride back home.

"You didn't have to do that. What a nice gesture." Dr. Hynes said. He was very thankful for the gift. "What could I tell you? I was brought up to be nice." Bert said sarcastically. "You may have had it rough, but my parents were no picnic either. They divorced when I was young. We lived on a farm back then. My father was known around the town as the walking toilet." Dr. Hynes said.

"Was it some kind of body odor problem? Those farmers do spend a lot of time around the animals." Bert inquired. "No, he didn't smell! He just took his share of shit from people. Wise ass!" Dr. Hynes said, as he cracked a smile.

"Why did they get divorced? You never told me."
Bert asked. "No, never mind that, you'll laugh at it."
Dr. Hynes said. "Oh come on. I won't laugh." Bert
said, as he took a sip of his soda. "Well, my father
caught my mother in bed with the cow salesman." Dr.
Hynes said, as Bert spit up a mouthful of soda all over
the windshield and choked from laughing.

Dr. Hynes lost control of the car and drove over
two lanes and off the shoulder into the grass and
stopped in a small ditch. Once the dust cleared Dr.
Hynes looked over at Bert. "I told you that you were
going to laugh." Dr. Hynes said. The two of them let
out uncontrollable laughter. "A cow salesman?" Bert
asked, as Dr. Hynes started to drive the car back onto
the highway.

"Well, he was the guy that came around to see if
we needed livestock. I called him the cow salesman."
Dr. Hynes explained. "That is beautiful, just beautiful.
I guess we know which one was really your father."
Bert said.

"What does that mean?" Dr. Hynes questioned.
"You couldn't be the son of a cow salesman, the way
you steer." Bert joked. "Yea, that was funny, cow,
steer, my driving. You are just hilarious. I would be
embarrassed to make a joke that bad." Dr. Hynes
replied while they continued to laugh and drive off.

The car was fine; there were just a few dings and
dirt marks. Nothing the local car wash couldn't fix up.

After being back in school for a couple of days,
Bert was walking across campus between classes. A
young lady named Kathryn approached him. Like
many of the other girls at the college, Kathryn was also
attracted to Bert.

"Hi Albert, I haven't seen you in a while, what's new?" she asked. "Not much Kathy, just the usual. How was your weekend?" Bert asked. "Pretty good, nothing exciting. So have they found out anything about your friend Stephanie yet?" Kathy asked.

"What do you mean, found anything out about?" Bert asked with a confused look on his face. "Oh no, you didn't know? I'm sorry." She said. "Know what? What is going on?" Bert excitedly asked.

Kathy pulled him over to a bench to sit down. "No one is really sure what happened. Someone reported her as missing. She hasn't been around for a while." Kathy informed him. Bert put his hands over his face and leaned forward to put his head down. "Oh my God. I can't believe this. Where was she last seen?" Bert asked.

"Like I said, no one is really sure of anything. There is a private investigator walking around questioning people. He said he was working with the police. I don't know how that works. He might be able to answer some of your questions though." Kathy said.

"Yes, if you see him get his number for me, I would like to talk to him." Bert said. "You bet, and if you need anyone to talk to or anything, you know where to find me. Hang in there Bert, hopefully everything will be fine." Kathy said. Bert seemed to take the news rather hard. That was expected since they were sort of dating, although they were not close enough to be referred to as a couple.

Bert tried to set up a meeting with the investigator. When he finally did meet with him; there wasn't much information to go on.

The investigator, Dennis, informed Bert that no one knew when she left, or if she decided to leave on her own. None of her family could be reached either. "You are just about the only one that has any concern about the subject. You would've been the one I'd be questioning if it hadn't been for the messages you left on her machine and all of the professors speaking so highly of you." Dennis explained.

"But please, isn't there anything we can do? Are you just going to give up?" Bert asked. "Look, I will keep your number and I will do my best to see what I can come up with but I'm telling you, it's not going to be easy. I'm sorry." Dennis said.

Bert pulled the charm out of his pocket and looked down at it with a sad look on his face. "What's that?" Dennis asked. "Just something I picked up for her over the weekend. I guess there are no games scheduled for today." Bert said. "What does that mean?" Dennis asked.

"My brother used to tell me that the best thing on a day off from school was to make a great big picture of iced tea, cook up a few hotdogs, get real comfortable and sit in front of the television to watch the games all day long. The saddest thing he ever imagined was preparing for a day like that and then reading in the paper that there are no games scheduled for today. So whenever I get upset about something, the words just come out." Bert explained.

Dennis looked at Bert again. "Once again, I am very sorry." He said, as he walked away shaking his head.

When Dennis got back to his shabby office, he couldn't stop thinking about Bert and how upset he looked about Stephanie. Dennis wished he could find some way to help.

Over the next few months Dennis tried every option he could come up with to find out what happened to Stephanie. He questioned every student at the college and looked into every place that anyone of them recommended he check out. He still came up with nothing.

September 1981

Dennis was finally able to locate Stephanie's parents. They were shocked to find out that their daughter has been missing. They haven't spoken with her since she left their house three years earlier.

Stephanie's parents explained to Dennis that they had a falling out about her choices before she decided to go to college. Her parents were unaware that she was even going to college.

Now, not only did Dennis feel terrible about how sad Bert was, but he also felt awful about Stephanie's parents and how they had to find out from him that she was missing.

Dennis eventually reported back to Bert to let him know how hard he tried. Bert was thankful, but by this time he figured that Stephanie would not be returning.

Bert was back to his studies and science experiments. He spent most of his time in his laboratory. When he wasn't working on his projects he would occasionally see Kathryn. Bert explained to Kathryn that he didn't want to get too serious with a woman at this point in his life, mainly because of his studies. He also let her know that even though

Stephanie and him only knew each other for a brief while, he still thinks of her often.

Bert stayed in contact with Dennis over the next few years. They became pretty close friends. Bert also made it up to Maine with Dr. Hynes a few more times and that is what inspired his next project.

G. Novitsky

Chapter Three
"Fear of Flying"

March 1989

Since Bert had so much land on his property he got to work on making a lake. He read up on, and studied the construction of tunnels. He built one under the length of the lake. Bert was determined to show the world that there could be a civilization built under the oceans. He spent quite a lot of time on this project as well as working on many other experiments at the same time.

Bert completed his tunnel experiment around the same time that he was graduating and receiving his doctorate degree. He brought Dr. Hynes and Dennis over to see the tunnel experiment and they were extremely impressed.

The only help Bert had building was from Carl Morris of the construction company. Carl was also very impressed with what Bert was attempting to do. Carl helped with the plumbing and electrical that was needed in order to live down there. Carl was convinced that Bert's idea would be a great thing to unveil to the public. Even if houses and living space were not built under the ocean, it would be a great place for certain types of businesses and things of that nature.

February 2003

A few years after Bert graduated and after the world knew of his experiments; he was invited back to

England to his former school to speak to the students and show some of his works. The school offered to fly him and a guest back to England and give them a place to stay for a week.

Bert was excited about the offer. Besides being able to teach the young minds, he figured this would also give him the opportunity to visit with his father and see his old home.

Bert decided to take Dr. Hynes with him. He figured it was the least he could do since Dr. Hynes brought him to that beautiful place in Maine so many times. Bert told Dr. Hynes about the trip and he was thrilled by the invitation.

They were flying out of Boston. Dennis gave them a ride to the airport. Bert invited Dennis also but he had a case that he was finishing up.

Bert and Dr. Hynes caught their flight early in the morning. After the take off, Dr. Hynes had a little nervousness in his stomach. This was the first time he was going to be on a plane for that many hours.

After a couple of hours in the sky, Dr. Hynes was not the only nervous one on the plane. Bert noticed out of the corner of his eye a man fidgeting around. The man started to make coughing sounds like he was trying to clear his throat. The man's friend turned to him to ask if he was all right. The man said yes, but it was obvious that he couldn't really speak.

The man got out of his seat and walked to the bathroom door, it was occupied. He walked back to his seat looking very nervous. He sat back down next to his friend again. After a second or two the man got back up and walked back to the bathroom.

He tried a different one this time and went inside. He was only in there for a minute or two before he walked back to his seat again. Bert noticed that the man was shaking a bit.

The man then walked back to the bathroom and went in once again. The man's friend looked quite confused and he didn't know what to do.

Bert got up and walked over to the man's friend. "What is your friend's name?" Bert asked. "George, why?" The man replied. "He needs comfort." Bert said back to him.

George came walking down the aisle once again and he looked like he was even more nervous than before. Bert walked towards him and stopped in front of him. "George? Oh my God. George, how are you?" Bert asked, as he hugged George very tight.

"Everything is going to be fine George. I had the same experience last year flying to The States from England. Once I realized that we would be landing in ten minutes it made it all go away and I was fine. What you need right now is a nice stiff drink, let me buy you one, and we can catch up on old times. Let's have a drink quickly because we will be landing soon. You look good George." Bert continued to whisper in George's ear as he motioned to the stewardess to bring the liquor cart.

George suddenly looked much better. "Where do I know you from?" George asked. "We went to the same school. What do you like to drink? Scotch?" Bert asked. "Yea, yea, let me have a scotch." George said.

The stewardess brought them two scotches. "Thanks sweetheart, keep them coming." Bert said.

Bert stayed with George for a little while before returning to Dr. Hynes.

"What was that all about?" Dr. Hynes asked. "That sir, was a classic case of a panic attack." Bert replied. "Yea, but who had one, him or you?" Dr. Hynes joked. "Funny." Bert replied. "How did you know? Where did you learn how to handle it?" Dr. Hynes asked.

"I did some studying on the subject. Airplanes are a common place for claustrophobia and panic attacks to come out. Most people who suffer from either one of them don't fly. I do have experience with hypnotism, but that alone couldn't have made him as comfortable as he became. He needed to feel safe and accepted. That's why I hugged him and told him that I had a similar experience recently." Bert went on.

"That was superb. I am glad that I was here to see your performance. Now let me buy you a drink." Dr. Hynes said. "No thank you, I didn't even want this one. You take it." Bert said. Dr. Hynes pointed to George "Take a look now." He said. George was fast asleep and his friend gave Bert a thumbs up.

The plane landed a few hours later. A couple of faculty members from the school were at the airport to greet Bert and Dr. Hynes. "Dr. Bleckard?" One of the teachers asked. "Yes, yes, call me Bert, and this is Arthur Hynes." Bert said. "A pleasure Mr. Hynes. Hello Bert. I am Thomas and this is my associate, Lynn." Thomas said.

"Very nice to meet you gentlemen." Lynn said. Thomas and Lynn helped them with their bags and showed them to the hotel where they would be staying.

The hotel room was very large and comfortable. Bert and Dr. Hynes were quite impressed. "Here is a number where I can be reached whenever you're ready Bert. Take your time and make yourself at home. After you are all settled in we can get together to discuss the agenda." Lynn said.

"You can reach me at that number also. Give me a ring if you would like to go down to the pub or something." Thomas said. "Sounds fantastic. We will give you a call later on. Thank you for everything." Bert said, as Dr. Hynes waved good bye.

G. Novitsky

Chapter Four
"You've got some case"

March 2003

Back in Boston, Dennis received a call from a woman who claimed that her daughter was being abused by her boyfriend. "I need your help. The police tell me I need proof before I can press any charges on something like this. What do they need, my daughters dead body? That's the only proof I'll be able to provide if I wait for them to help me." The woman said frantically.

"Okay ma'am, just calm down. I will help you. Where can we meet?" Dennis asked. "I live off of Salem Street near route sixteen." The woman said. Dennis made arrangements to meet the woman for coffee in a donut shop on Riverside Avenue.

Dennis walked into the shop and he noticed a nervous woman sitting in a corner booth. "I believe you called me." Dennis said. "What makes you think that?" The woman asked. "Let's just say, I can place a face to a voice." Dennis said. "That's good enough for me. I was just testing to see how good of an investigator you are." The woman said. "Does this mean I passed? The name is Dennis." He said, as he reached out to shake her hand.

"Oh, I'm Rosa. Nice to meet you." Rosa said, as she shook his hand. She was very pretty. She had long dark hair and nice, soft, tan skin. She was close to five foot six at about one hundred and fifteen pounds, which was distributed nicely.

Dennis tried not to let her know that he noticed how attractive she was. He didn't like to mix business and pleasure. He liked to stay professional when he was on a case.

"So, you think some guy is smacking your daughter around?" Dennis bluntly asked. "That's why I called you. My daughter Amy has been dating this bastard for almost a year now. I didn't like it since the beginning. The last few times I saw her, she was making excuses. One was for her limp and the others for bruises." Rosa said.

"How did you hear about me?" Dennis asked. "Funny you should ask. I called another organization and the girl that answers the phones there recommended you." Rosa said. "Oh, how nice. Well, you said she was making excuses, what were some of those?" Dennis asked.

"Well, for her limp she told me that she banged her knee on the car door. I found out that was bullshit when I noticed that she could bend her knee fine. The damage was actually in her thigh. Her black eye, She blamed that on the refrigerator door. That was a half ass excuse if I ever heard one. I also noticed some black and blues on both of her arms and for a girl that always wore short sleeved shirts to suddenly stop, that also led me to believe that she was hiding something." Rosa went on.

"It looks to me that you have every right to believe that she is being mistreated. Let me just tell you that the cops are not totally wrong by not investigating it completely though. I have seen many cases where girls are being abused or beaten and then when it comes down to it, they choose to stay with the scumbags that are inflicting harm on them. If this is what is going on though, you can be sure that I will provide all of the proof that you need. I just hope that you will be able to handle it when I show you." Dennis said.

"I will handle it fine. When it comes down to her making a choice, I will be the one making it for her. You bring me everything you can find on this guy. Don't worry about her making a bad decision, seeing him was her last bad decision." Rosa stated.

Dennis took down all of the information that he needed to begin looking into the boyfriend, Rick.

Back in England, Bert was in the middle of showing the children around the lab. He explained what he does as a scientist and he gave them access to the equipment so that the kids could work on their own projects.

While the kids were putting together some experiments, Bert was talking to Lynn. "So, later on tonight some of us will be stopping by the pub, will you and Arthur be joining us tonight?" Lynn asked. "Yes, you can count on us tonight. I was just worried about keeping up my end of the bargain, meeting with the children and showing them some things. Now that we made it through that without any problems." Bert was saying, as all of a sudden there was a big crash and explosion in the back of the classroom.

One of the children was mixing some formulas and he bumped the table and all of the beakers and mixtures fell to the floor and caused an explosion. The children were stunned but unharmed. The explosion caused a fire in the back of the room.

Bert and Lynn got all of the students out of the room. Lynn called the fire department as Bert attacked the fire with the extinguisher. Bert couldn't put the fire out. It ended up becoming an uncontrollable blaze.

The classroom next door got the worst of it. Luckily all of the students were brought to safety in time.

The fire department arrived and after an hour and a half of grueling work, the fire was finally out. Bert seemed very embarrassed that this happened while he was instructing.

Later on that evening Bert kept his promise. He and Dr. Hynes met Lynn and the other faculty members at the pub. "Uh oh, get the fire extinguisher, here he comes." Thomas said, as Bert walked in. Bert walked over and shook hands with everyone in the group while laughing. "Yes, that was some scene. I am just glad that I could entertain all of you. You all remember Dr. Hynes?" Bert said as he pointed out that Dr. Hynes was with him.

Everyone started to loosen up and have a good time. Lynn told Bert how impressed she was with all that he accomplished over the past few years. The two of them got to talking and Bert invited her to stay with him if she could ever make it to The States. He thought that she would make a good partner for upcoming science projects.

Lynn was very interested in the invitation. She told him that he could count on seeing her there. By the end of the night they exchanged phone numbers and looked forward to seeing each other in the future.

The next day Bert went to see his old house. He knocked on the door and his brother answered. It was an awkward moment for the both of them. They had some differences before his brother moved to The States.

They did the mature thing and put those differences aside. Bert reached out his hand and his brother shook it. "So, you came back from The States?" Bert asked.

"Yea, I came back home in eighty seven. The States weren't really the place for me. It took thirteen years to figure that out. I was enjoying some of it but I ran into some trouble and the only way to get out of it was to run home to dad." His brother said.

"I won't even ask about it. I am just happy to see that you got away from whatever it was. How is old daddy, anyway?" Bert asked. "He is doing pretty good, he was sober for twenty days." His brother said with a smile.

"Really? That is wonderful. I am proud of him." Bert said. "Don't be too proud, those twenty days were not consecutive." His brother replied, as they both let out a laugh. "So, the old goat is still polishing off the bottles?" Bert inquired.

"No actually he is much better since the accident." His brother said. "Tell me you're joking again. What accident?" Bert asked.

Bert's brother explained how their father had too much to drink a couple of years ago in the local pub. He started mouthing off as he normally did after putting a load on. This time someone heard enough and waited for him outside of the bar until closing time. The man took a crow bar to their father's knee and shattered it. It took him over a year to be able to walk again. Since the surgery he walks with a cane.

It turned out that the man who did it was an old acquaintance of Bert's. It was a man named Scott, someone who cursed Bert many years earlier for carrying a satanic bible.

Bert spent his last night in England eating dinner with his brother and father. They made their peace with one another and enjoyed the reunion.

When Bert returned home he played back several messages on his voice mail from Dennis. He gave Dennis a call to find out what has been going on. He just wanted to tell him about the situation that Rosa needed corrected.

He informed Bert of all the details and asked him if he would like to tag along on the investigation. Dennis wanted some company, he also figured that Bert would probably be a big help.

Bert told Dennis that he would enjoy accompanying him. He felt that it might be a bit exciting.

The two of them met in Dennis' office. "I see the cleaning lady is still on vacation." Bert joked, as he looked around the messy room. "Oh yea, I've been meaning to give her a call but I can't seem to find her number." Dennis joked back, as he looked under a pile of scattered papers.

"So, where does this little adventure begin?" Bert asked. "Well, I have the address right here. I think this guy hangs out with some kind of gang-bangers or something like that. You may get that excitement you wanted." Dennis said.

"That may be a little more than I was expecting." Bert stated. "You really don't have to come along if you don't want to. If it makes you feel better though, nothing will be happening on this trip. I just want to get a feel for who this guy is. We will probably just tail him around for a little while and maybe take a couple of pictures." Dennis said.

"Do whatever you have to do, I'm with you. I could use a little action in my life. It will even out all of the studying and research I am used to." Bert said.

They arrived at the apartment that Rosa told Dennis about. They sat in the car outside for about an hour when finally a speeding car pulled up the block. The car stopped short in front of the apartment building and parked half in the street and half on the sidewalk. A young thug got out of the car and he walked to the front door of the apartment building.

"Is that your friend?" Bert asked. "No, I don't think so. Rosa described him to be different. Not much different, but I don't think that is him." Dennis said.

A short while later the thug came walking out of the building with another young guy with the same type of look. "That's my friend." Dennis said. "Are you sure?" Bert asked. "That is who Rosa described to me. Slim, ugly, arrogant looking piece of crap." Dennis recalled.

"That describes both of them." Bert commented. "Slim, ugly, arrogant looking piece of crap, with a dirty little beard." Dennis corrected himself. "Oh, okay, then that's your friend." Bert said.

The two of them got into the car and the driver started it up. The rear wheels spun as dirt and smoke filled the air around the rear of the car. Then they sped off. Dennis started his car and followed a safe distance behind them.

"Do you always get yourself mixed up in this type of stuff?" Bert asked. "It comes with the territory." Dennis said, as he smirked.

"Should I be taking some snapshots?" Bert asked. "Wait until they stop, and then maybe you could get some good shots of their faces." Dennis said. "I seen their faces, and they certainly wouldn't make good shots." Bert joked.

"Yea, these guys don't have the most attractive looks, but for some reason the girls these days are into that scumbag image. These two slobs aren't the worst I've seen though. I have been on many cases with a number of interesting characters." Dennis said, as he began to describe some of the strange people that he runs into in his line of work.

"Oh, I guess it's time to eat." Bert interrupted, as he pointed at the guys pulling into a drive thru McDonald's. "Kids these days don't know what things are about. They should just find the one thing that gives them true happiness and stick with it." Bert commented. "That's an easy choice for me, Skynard makes me happy." Dennis replied, as he raised the radio volume.

He pulled to the side of the road across the street from the McDonald's. After the guys placed their order they drove around to the first window. There were two windows. The first one was to pay and the second one was to pick up the food.

"What the hell is he doing?" Dennis asked. The driver pulled the attendants arm out of the drive up window and he had him dangling. Rick made his way around the car from the passenger side and reached in to clean out the register.

Dennis got on his phone and called the local police. He had all of the phone numbers he needed because of his line of work.

Rick got back into the car and they sped off with the rear wheels screeching once again, as they left the attendant lying outside of the window.

Dennis followed them as he informed the police over the phone of every move they made. After a few blocks, a police unit turned down the street with the sirens blaring. The thieves noticed the police and made a quick U-turn, almost crashing into several other cars on the road. They made a quick right turn and Rick bailed out of the car.

The police didn't see him get out. They continued to chase the car for a few more blocks until another police unit pulled out in front of the car. They boxed the driver in. The officers got out of their cars with guns drawn. They made the driver show his hands as they moved toward the car to pull him out.

The driver was taken in for resisting arrest, robbery, and possession of a weapon. There were two guns found in the car. Rick wasn't quick enough to take the weapons but he was able to make it off with the cash.

The police locked the driver up. His name was Kevin Lawrence, but he went by his middle name, David. He only lived in the area for a short while. He bounced around from city to city.

It turned out that he was not in the same age group as most of the kids he hung around with. He was in his thirties. He never grew up. He bragged to his cellmate how he was running around with guns all of his life.

The two of them got to talking and David shared some of his stories. "I'm a lot smarter than I used to be." David informed the man. "What do you mean?" The man asked.

"Do you want to hear something stupid I did back in the eighties when I committed my first crime? I was only a teenager then. I was living in Detroit at the time. I held up an older couple. The man started to put up a fight. I ended up shooting him in the leg and running. I ditched my gun behind some garbage pails and I split." David said.

"That does sound pretty dumb." The man commented. "That wasn't the dumb part. See, I loved that gun. It was my first one. It was nice and small and it had a really cool looking red handle. I liked it so much I decided to put my initials on it. There it was, lying behind some trash cans with a big K.D.L. on it." David explained.

"That is even less intelligent." The man said. "You're telling me. I was just lucky that I left Detroit without a record. They never nailed me for that one, thank God. Do you know how embarrassing that would have been? The point is, if you plan on being a thief, it's not too smart to label your piece with your initials." David explained.

"Thanks for the tip. I'll have to remember that." The man said sarcastically. "Why are you here?" David asked.

"I'm here because I helped out a friend. You see, where I come from, friends watch each other's backs. I would ask you if you had time for a story but obviously, you do.

My friend has a couple of young kids. He just bought them one of those basketball hoops that you put out by your sidewalk. Anyway, he has this real useless piece of shit neighbor that has been starting trouble ever since they had a senseless disagreement about a fence.

My friend put this basketball stand and hoop together, which is another whole story. It took a while but he finally put it together and set it up on the strip of grass by the sidewalk between his house and his wonderful neighbor's house.

My friend took his family out for dinner and when he got home, his wife noticed the hoop had been moved and it had a nasty note on it from this asshole neighbor. He was upset because he thought that the wonderful lawn, that wasn't even his, might have gotten a little messy.

My friend's wife was annoyed by it and she moved the hoop back to where it was. Later that night while my friend was sleeping, the hoop was moved again. His wife was awake and she moved it back again, hoping to have a word with the coward next door. A short while later it happened again and his wife and the piece of garbage neighbor got into words.

The neighbor was yelling at the top of his lungs a list of unintelligible words describing how much he adored his grass. I tell you, it's a damn shame that asshole didn't care half as much for his dog as he did for his grass. The poor dog is locked in an outdoor jail all year round in all kinds of horrible weather. That too is another story.

Now picture a grown man, running out of his house to push a child's toy around. Pretty friggen pathetic huh? Well, this moron was so enraged his senseless screaming woke up my friend and the kids.

The kids were hysterical crying, thinking their mother was going to be hurt by this asshole. He was hollering that he was calling the cops. My friend's wife told him to please do so.

A short while later the police showed up. They went to the genius's house first and they had a hard time conversing with him due to his ramblings of anger and stupidity. The police then visited my friend and his wife, they had a nice, long, peaceful, intelligent conversation about the ridiculousness of the jerk off next door.

The next day, the idiot was not finished. He took it upon himself to drive steel spikes into the ground sticking up close to a foot high. This was his clever idea of a property line. Now anyone with the smallest level of common sense would realize that these things could possibly hurt someone.

Luckily, an older, wiser neighbor stepped forward and confronted this pinhead about the situation. The pinhead then proceeded to take his spikes and walk off with his tail between his legs, realizing his foolish decision. Are you still awake David?" The man asked.

"Yes, yes what happened next? You have my interest." David replied, as the man continued his story. "So I was so pissed off after hearing the whole story that I sat outside that guys house waiting for him to come home the next day. He pulled into his driveway and I got out of my car. I told him to hold up a second.

He stepped toward me and I cracked him in the mouth as hard as I could. When he went down he banged his head on the cement and I kicked him in the ribs for a short while and broke a couple. I dragged him to his dog's jail and put him in and took the dog out and I locked it. Then I drove off.

Well, the first person to be questioned was my friend and I wasn't going to let him go down for something I did. I took my punishment. Let me tell you something, I would do it all over again in a second.

If I didn't do what I did, this scumbag would never have seen justice. And believe me, four broken ribs and a jaw wired shut is damn sweet justice! The best part is, this asshole doesn't even know me, and the guy I did it for can look at him and laugh when he sees him. That asshole will think again before he starts pushing kids toys around and making them cry.

Like I said, where I come from, friends stick together. It's better than waiting to catch a prick like this on camera screwing with your property so he can get a ten dollar fine." The man said.

David enjoyed the story to a point. He was unreasonable like the neighbor in the story and he didn't care about making kids cry or breaking their toys. He also would kick a dog for standing in his way, and he didn't have a problem with screaming at a defenseless woman without a reason. He would do that any day of the week.

David and his gang were known in their neighborhood for being heartless. David was going to share another story with the man but when he realized the man had decency, he kept that story to himself. It was about a girl in his neighborhood who was very excited about her engagement.

The girl and her husband to be, wanted to go all out for their wedding. They put every penny they had toward it. They spent weeks waiting to get their invitations from the printers. They finally finished writing all of them, close to two hundred, and then they walked down the block to mail them as one of David's gang members watched them.

David's pal waited until all of the invitations were in the mailbox and the couple walked back to the house. Then he walked to the side of the house closest to the mailbox and pulled out their garden hose. He placed the end of the hose into the mailbox and then he turned the water on and let it run until someone discovered it the next morning.

The couple didn't know about the invitations being destroyed until two weeks later. That event showed how warm hearted this gang was.

A guard walked over to the cell and brought David out to question him about his accomplice that got away.

Bert and Dennis headed back to Rosa's daughter's apartment to see if Rick was going to return.

Eventually Amy walked out of the building. She stood outside for a few minutes until another car pulled up. Another guy was driving it. Amy walked over and got into the car. Dennis took some pictures of them before they drove off.

"What do you make of that?" Dennis asked. "Maybe that guy is the reason she is getting beaten." Bert answered. "Or maybe that guy is giving the beatings." Dennis remarked.

Dennis started the car and followed them. They drove around for a little while until the couple pulled into a quiet secluded spot. It was sort of a parking lot, except there weren't any cars around.

Trees and shrubbery surrounded the area. It would have been a nice place to relax if the gangsters didn't deface it. They hung around there at night and destroyed it with their ugly graffiti.

Dennis parked some distance away from them. It was a difficult area to get close to. From what Dennis could make out, the couple seemed to be hugging and kissing. "All right, we're going to get a little show." Bert joked.

They looked on for a short while, when suddenly things started to appear a bit violent. They could only see the guy's hands waving around aggressively. Amy got out of the car and started to walk away. Dennis began to snap some pictures, one after the other.

The guy got out of the car and chased her down. They started arguing very loudly. He grabbed her by the back of her head and threw her to the ground. She lied there crying, as Dennis continued to snap away.

"Do you want to stay here? Do you want to lie here and cry? Maybe I'm not done beating your ass, bitch! Get your ass back in the car! Now! Bitch!" He yelled, as he picked her back up by her hair and brought her back to the car and threw her in.

They sat there a little while longer before he started up the car and drove off. Dennis followed them back to the apartment, staying far enough behind not to blow his cover, now that he has a case building.

Amy was dropped off in front of her apartment. She ran inside with her hands covering her face as the guy sped away.

"Are you up for more?" Dennis asked Bert. "I guess so. You have to do your job, right? I'm not going to take you away from that. Besides, this is starting to get interesting." Bert answered.

Dennis pulled away once again and followed the guy back to where he lives. "I hope you don't think of it as cruel that I have to sit and watch these things and not help the victims." Dennis said. "I understand completely. You wouldn't be able to provide good information to your clients if you interfered. Not to mention, you could be killed." Bert said, as he let out a small laugh.

"I'm glad you understand. I'm not crazy about these kinds of cases. They are exciting but I would much rather investigate something less violent." Dennis said. "I know what you mean but you have to take the jobs that are going to pay the bills. Besides, there aren't going to be any church's calling you to investigate." Bert joked.

The guy got out of his car and walked into the side entrance to a run down, small, beat up shack. Dennis and Bert sat outside for a short while until they were convinced that the guy was staying in for the night. "I guess we got enough for one day." Dennis said.

"Sounds good. I have that speech to make tomorrow night at the award ceremony. It will be nice to get some rest and prepare. You're going to be there, right?" Bert asked. "I wouldn't miss it for the world." Dennis said.

The next day was the day that Bert accepted his award for scientific accomplishments and he mentioned during his speech that he had a very big announcement to make very soon.

When he finished his speech, Bert walked off the stage and Dennis and Dr. Hynes greeted him. "You just had to mention being on an undercover case. Didn't you?" Dennis joked. "Well done old boy. So, you have been keeping a secret from even your closest friends?" Dr. Hynes asked.

"I was worried about you guys asking for an explanation. Well, here it is. I want you to wait like everyone else. This way it will be as perfect as I planned." Bert said.

"I knew we would get some kind of run around like that." Dennis said. "Oh well. We will let you have your little secret but you have to come celebrate with us tonight." Dr. Hynes insisted.

"That sounds good. I'll take you up on that." Bert said. They all went with some others from the ceremony to a restaurant down the road.

After dinner, they stayed at the bar for drinks. Even Bert loosened up and had a few, which was not like him. The other guys joked about getting him drunk so they could get the secret out of him.

Dennis began to talk to Bert about the investigation and he showed him the pictures that they took the previous day. "Oh wow, these came out nice. That is some camera you got. Hey, do you mind if I hold on to a couple of these?" Bert asked. "I guess not, I have doubles. Should I ask why?" Dennis asked.

"I feel like I am your partner on this case, just let me hold a few." Bert insisted. "Sure, why not? I guess it couldn't hurt. Just don't show them around." Dennis said, as Bert picked out the ones he liked and tucked them into his jacket pocket.

Dennis spent the next couple of days following Amy and her boyfriend, Rick around. It became clear to him that Rick was not the one leaving the marks on her. It was the other guy acting on his own.

Once he was convinced of that, Dennis paid a visit to Rosa. He explained the situation to her and also showed her the pictures of her daughter being thrown around near the guy's car. He also explained that even though her boyfriend was not beating her, he is still a piece of garbage criminal that she should stay away from.

Rosa didn't need much convincing of that. She informed Dennis that she has a cousin who lives down in South Carolina in a nice quiet section. She was thinking about packing her daughter up and moving down there with her.

Dennis was a bit surprised that the situation was going to cause Rosa to make such a drastic change of life. He also felt that it was a pretty good idea to remove her daughter from the self-destruction she chose to take on.

Dennis and Rosa began spending much more time together. She needed someone to talk to at this point in her life and Dennis was a good listener.

After a couple of weeks Rosa decided that she was definitely ready to head down south. Dennis was the first one she called to tell the news to.

"So, you're really going to do it? I'm proud of you. That is a big decision to make. It takes a lot of balls. I mean, you know what I mean." Dennis tripped over his words.

"Thanks, and I think we are close enough to say words like balls. Don't be shy. It wasn't an easy choice to make but I think it's the right one. My cousin told me that she could set me up with some part time work. She also has spare rooms for Amy and me to use until we get set up. I am kind of excited about it. You know, starting over and all. I don't have to tell you about the weather down there. It's going to be like spring all year round." Rosa went on.

"Like I said, I am very happy for you. If you need any help, just let me know." Dennis said. "Well, I would like you to see the place, maybe you could take a ride and help us move in? I'll pay you." Rosa suggested.

"If you plan it for a week that I'm free, I'll be glad to lend you a hand. "Dennis said. Rosa and Dennis worked out the details and they set up a date where Dennis would be available to help.

G. Novitsky

Chapter Five
"The Move"

April 2003

It was a bright sunny Friday morning. Dennis got out of bed at seven thirty AM. He yawned and stretched his arms out as he glanced out of his bedroom window towards the sunrise. "What a beautiful morning for a drive down south." He said to himself.

After he showered and got dressed, he gave Bert a call to see if he would change his mind and come for the trip. He asked him before but Bert just said that he would get back to him on it.

"It sounds like a lot of fun but I am really busy over here right now. I'll tell you what, once you two start dating and you go back down there, I promise I will make time then." Bert said.

"Real funny. What makes you think I'll be dating her?" Dennis asked. "Some things you can just tell." Bert replied.

Dennis cracked a smile and told Bert to just go and get his work done. "I will, you just enjoy your trip and let the romance work itself out." Bert said, as they ended the call.

Dennis arrived at Rosa's apartment just after nine o'clock with two coffees. Rosa and Amy already had the U-haul filled and ready to go. Dennis drove the truck and they let Amy drive Dennis' car for the beginning of the trip. They figured that would give her some needed time to herself.

Dennis and Rosa talked about how nice the new town was going to be. Dennis was thinking about how Bert mentioned him dating Rosa and he felt a slight bit of nervousness in his stomach. He did his best to hide it until they reached the first rest area. He was able to get a hold of himself as the three of them ate together.

While they were at the rest area Amy asked her mother to join her in Dennis' car for the next portion of the trip. Dennis enjoyed Rosa's company in the truck but driving by himself helped him remain calm.

A few hours later they arrived at Rosa's cousin Linda's house. Linda was very excited to see Rosa and Amy. They spent a while getting reacquainted. She also welcomed Dennis to the house and he made himself comfortable in the TV room while the girls caught up.

Linda had a big dinner prepared for all of them. Over dinner they got on the subject of Dennis' occupation. "So, I hear you have an exciting job Dennis." Linda inquired. "I guess you could say it has its moments." Dennis said as he smirked.

"It's too bad you don't have an office in this neighborhood. There is some pretty strange stuff that should be investigated around here." Linda said. "Really? What could be happening down here?" Rosa asked.

"Well, there are some pretty strange things happening on the other side of town. I guess you can say it has to do with devil worship." Linda explained.

"Wow, maybe this town does have some excitement!" Amy exclaimed. "Easy Amy, you are not getting involved in that evilness." Rosa said in a protective tone.

"Do you know any of the details of this thing? Even if I don't live here, something like this could make for interesting work." Dennis inquired. "I don't have all of the details but some friends of mine tell me that it has something to do with the church of St. Barabus across town. Recently the people of the Parish have just seemed to change. They say there is an evil darkness about them now. I stay away from that side of town since I heard." Linda explained.

Dennis spent the night on the couch in Linda's TV room. He tossed and turned all night thinking about the church. Very quietly in the early morning hours he buttered himself a bagel and left a note for Rosa explaining that he had to get an early start home. He left the house and decided to pay a visit to the church.

G. Novitsky

Chapter Six
"Enter the Church"

Dennis walked into the church through the main doors. He felt a dark coldness about the room. It wasn't like any church he had ever been in before. He glanced around at the stained glass windows. The pictures resembled any of those in other churches except for minor changes made to them.

He noticed an older woman kneeling in front of the candles. He walked closer to her as she took notice of him. "Good morning young man." The woman said, as she took his hand into hers and looked deep into his eyes. There was something about her eyes that made Dennis feel like she was pulling him in.

"Good morning. I'm sorry to interrupt your prayers, I was just looking around." Dennis said. "Don't be silly. It is always nice to meet a fellow churchgoer. Are you considering joining our parish?" The woman asked.

"Well, maybe, you see, I'm just in town visiting a friend. I was passing by and I thought I would take a look around." Dennis explained.

"What do you think? Do you like our church?" She asked. "Yes, yes. It is very nice. It's catholic right?" Dennis asked. "Why of course it's catholic. What religion are you a follower of?" The woman asked. "Oh, I'm also catholic. It has just been such a long time since I have been in church." Dennis said.

"A good catholic shouldn't stray from the church. This is where all of your strength comes from. You should stay for a mass and get yourself reacquainted." She suggested.

"That's a good idea. When are the masses?" He asked. "Sundays of course. You have been away too long. You should come to the twelve-noon mass tomorrow. Father Servat, our pastor always gives the twelve o'clock mass. You will get a lot from one of his sermons." The woman said.

"I will think about that. I may not be here tomorrow though, but I will keep it in mind for another Sunday." Dennis said. "Oh, you'll be here tomorrow, no one can turn down the church. I will look for you." The woman said, as she walked away.

Dennis left and he headed for the highway to go back home. He started to change the radio station as he noticed the on ramp to the highway on the right hand side. He looked over his shoulder to change lanes and he noticed one of Amy's bags sitting in the back. He figured he had to turn around and bring it back to her.

Rosa just started cooking some breakfast for Linda and Amy as a kind gesture for the hospitality she received. She noticed the note that Dennis had written. It said that he was sorry that he had to leave without saying goodbye, but he figured since he was up he should get an early start. She was upset that he was in such a hurry to leave.

Linda came down the stairs. "Wow, something smells really good. I wasn't expecting a gourmet breakfast." She said, as she sat down at the kitchen table and Rosa put a cup of coffee in front of her.

"It's the least I could do for you." Rosa said. "So where's your boyfriend Dennis? Still sleeping?" Linda asked. "No, he had to get an early start for the trip back home. He left a note." Rosa said, as she held up the piece of paper.

"Oh, that's too bad. I would've liked for him to hang around. I like him, What about you? Do you have an interest in him? It looks like he has one in you. Driving all the way down here for you." Linda said.

"Well, I see it this way." Rosa started to say, as there was a knock on the front door. "Hold that thought, let me get the door, but you are going to finish telling me whatever you were about to start." She said, as she went to answer the door.

Dennis was standing at the door holding the bag that was left behind. "I couldn't very well leave knowing that I was holding one of Amy's bags." He said. "That is very nice of you. Now you are coming in for some coffee. Look who couldn't stay away!" Linda yelled into the kitchen. Rosa had a smile of relief.

They all sat down and talked for a while. Dennis told them that he stopped by that church to see what it was all about. He told them that it gave off a very eerie feeling.

Linda talked Dennis into staying over for another night, since he didn't have to get back just yet. "We'll all go out and have a good time." She said.

During the course of the day Dennis tried to contact Bert over the phone. He wanted to see how things were back home. He just kept getting his machine. He figured Bert was into one of his projects.

Later that evening Dennis, Rosa and Linda went out for dinner and drinks. Amy said she would just rather stay in and rest and watch some television. Linda gave Amy her cell phone number and Rosa told her to call if she changed her mind or if she needed anything.

Linda brought them out to a Mexican restaurant that she goes to once in a while. She knew most of the people that worked there. "The usual table senorita?" The waiter asked.

"Si, Carlos, gracias." Linda replied. She knew some Spanish from her high school days. The only time she was able to use it was at the restaurant. Carlos showed them to their table in the corner by the window.

Over their wonderful dinner they got into a conversation about Bert. "So, your friend couldn't get away from his science projects for the weekend, huh?" Linda asked.

"He gets me a little worried sometimes. Did I tell you how he lost his mother when he was only eleven years old?" Dennis asked. "I think you mentioned it, Lupus right?" Rosa answered.

"Yea, he goes into these trances, or whatever you want to call them. He talks about how he can find a cure for the disease but he would be killed because of all of the revenue the medications bring in." Dennis explained.

"Is that really true? I heard many times how all or most illnesses can be cured but if they were, the medical industry would miss out on millions and millions of dollars from selling their medications and unnecessary patient visits." Linda asked.

"According to Bert, that is all true. I believe it. This sick world is bent on making a dollar. A few hundred thousand people having to be on medication all of their life or taking a shot everyday or hating what they look at in the mirror every morning is worth it to them I guess.

The good old dollar, do you realize that it was supposed to be one of the biggest honors to have your face on currency? Imagine what George Washington would say if he knew his picture was on every single evil dollar in the country. You would think there would be a picture of a red guy with horns on the dollar bill. Sorry, was I rambling?" Dennis went on.

"No, you make a lot of sense." Linda said. "Not me, I heard most of that talk from Bert. He said that he would rather find a cure for the world than the disease. He says that Lupus reminds him of the way the people in this country destroy one another and it's probably not worth finding cures for all of the illnesses because it would just make people healthier to go out and destroy each other with more ease." Dennis explained.

"I would probably be sent to the nut house if I spent all of that time looking into something that killed one of my parents." Rosa said. "Oh, the nut house. I don't think I would last two days in one of those places." Dennis said, as Carlos brought the check over.

"You no like de nut house? You no like work here." Carlos chimed in, as the whole table let out a laugh.

After a delightful dinner, Linda suggested going to a club down the block. Rosa called Amy to make sure everything was okay and asked her if she was interested in going to the club with them. "You guys have a good time. I am enjoying my quiet time, but thanks anyway." She said. "Okay sweetheart, just call if you need anything." Rosa replied.

Dennis was a little worried about what the club was going to be like. After they all had a few drinks and loosened up he explained why. "I was under the impression that this was going to be like the loud irritating places that my friends used to drag me to." He said.

"I know what places you're talking about. I am not crazy about them either, so crowded and sweaty. I remember trying to walk through the dance floor, I felt like a doghouse. Everyone trying to bury their bones in my backyard, if you get my point." Linda said.

Dennis and Rosa started to laugh. "Exactly, all those gorillas trying to get those club skanks in their Iroc's and Monte Carlo's for a quickie. I'm sorry, we used to call them club skanks." Dennis said, as he smirked.

"Don't worry, we used to call them worse things than that. They needed mini fire extinguishers in their purses in case their hair spray caught on fire when lighting their Marlboro lights." Linda said, as they all laughed again.

"It seemed the more the guy resembled an ape, the more club skanks he would get. I think those guys wore all those rings just so their knuckles wouldn't get scraped on the ground when they walked." Dennis said, as Rosa grabbed the table and held her wine in her mouth trying not to spit it up from laughing.

They continued to make jokes and have a great time. Dennis commented that he was thankful the girls could go out and listen to some rock and roll oldies and have a good time. That was his idea of fun.

When they returned to Linda's house they saw Amy sitting in the living room with her hands over her face crying. Rosa rushed over to see what was wrong.

"I know I wasn't supposed to call him. I know you're against me talking to him, but you won't have to worry about that anymore." Amy said while wiping her eyes.

"What do you mean? You called Rick?" Rosa asked. "Yes I did. I missed him." She said. "Why are you crying?" Rosa asked. "Because he is dead. He was shot tonight." She said, as tears rolled down her face.

"Oh my God!" Rosa reacted, as she held her daughter in her arms and rocked her back and forth. "He's gone." Amy said. "I am so sorry, I know it is rough to hear news like this." Rosa said as she tried to convince Amy that getting away from those people was the best thing for her. Rosa also explained that she is thankful that she took her away before something like this happened to her.

It took Rosa a couple of hours and a box of tissues to get Amy to finally go to sleep. When she was sleeping Rosa stayed up talking to Dennis about the situation. Dennis was very caring and he insisted that Rosa made the best decision to begin a new life for Amy. Rosa felt much better after speaking with him.

As it turned out, the woman from the church was right. Dennis made it to the twelve o'clock mass the next day. Father Servat performed the ceremony, just as the woman said he would. Father Servat looked no older than thirty years old. He was a tall thin man with a stern look about him. He quoted many parts of the bible, but he put a different type of spin on them.

He sounded as if he was claiming that God is someone other than the Catholic's believe him to be. Dennis could not be sure after one visit if it was devil worship. He was sure that it wasn't Catholicism though.

On his way out, towards the end of the mass, Dennis noticed the woman from the previous day standing in the rear section of the church. She gave him a look, as if she was telling him that she knew he would return. That gave him a strange feeling, as if he was walking in slow motion. He looked around as if he was dreaming and everyone just appeared to look dark and evil. He couldn't get out of there fast enough.

When he finally made it out of the doors, he had a great feeling of relief. He was the first one out because he left before it was over. On his way to the parking lot to find his car, he noticed a woman standing there looking at him as if he was some kind of a criminal.

Normally Dennis wouldn't confront someone on the street but something about this time made him curious. "Did I do something wrong ma'am?" He asked the woman. "You tell me." She responded. "What does that mean?" He asked. "You just walked out of the house of Satan and you're going to question if you did something wrong?" The woman asked.

"You know, you're the second one to say something like that about this place. Why do people think the devil operates from here?" Dennis asked.

"Did you take notice of all of the possessed eyes around you in there?" She asked. "I noticed they were different but I was trying to focus on what the Pastor was saying. I wanted to see if there really were any hidden evil messages in his mass. That is the only reason I came here." Dennis explained.

"So, Mr. investigative reporter, what did you find?" She asked sarcastically. "I can tell you that it is strange compared to any other religious ceremony I have attended, and yes, I am only here to investigate." Dennis said.

"Well let me just warn you not to become a frequent visitor. Some of those people in there used to be close friends of mine, in fact, I used to go to that church until that Father Lucifer started his brainwashing in there. He took the Lord out of my friends and replaced him with evilness." The woman stated.

"Is that why you stand out here? To inform people of the evil?" Dennis asked sarcastically. "Well, what agency are you from? I reported this place to the police a number of times and all I got from that was some smart mouth cop telling me that I am probably the problem." She went on.

The woman informed Dennis about her meeting with the police officer. She said that he went to watch the Pastor at a mass and he reported back to her saying that this priest was just like any other one. He says something and then the people repeat it. He tells them to stand and they stand. He tells them to sit and they sit. He tells them to kneel and they kneel. He explained to her that all religion is a form of brainwashing to him, so if he were to arrest this man for it, he would have to arrest every Rabbi, Priest, and Reverend in the state.

"Well I guess that cop had an obvious opinion on the subject. He did have a point. Look, I don't live around here. I just wanted to get an idea of what was going on, in case anyone ever did want an investigator." Dennis said.

"In that case, you have a group that would be interested in hiring you." The woman said. It turned out that the woman was part of a small group from the neighborhood that was interested in putting a stop to what went on at the church.

Dennis gave the woman his business card and told her that he would make some time to get a case together and she should give him a call when her group is ready to move forward.

He went back to Linda's house after that conversation to say his good-bye's and let them know that he would be in touch soon.

Chapter Seven
"Back at Home"

May 2003

When Dennis arrived back in New England, he was finally able to meet up with Bert. He had been working on selling one of his latest inventions.

"Is this one a secret also?" Dennis asked. "No, by no means. Let me explain it to you. Do you know what a pain in the ass it is around here during the huge snow storms?" Bert asked. "Yes, of course I do." Dennis answered. "Well, the last time I had to shovel I asked myself, how come nobody put a stop to this aggravation yet? Then I came up with an idea." Dennis stated, as he pulled out a small plastic type carpet.

"What is that? It doesn't look like a shovel." Dennis joked. Bert unrolled it on the ground and plugged it in. "See, it's waterproof. You put it down before it snows and plug it in. It heats up and any snow that falls on it melts before it can accumulate. You put them anywhere you don't want to shovel." Bert explained.

"That is friggen ingenious. How come no one ever thought of that?" Dennis asked. "I am sure someone asked that same question to the guy who introduced the snow blower. It gets better. The people I sold the idea to mentioned larger ones for on top of buildings. No more roofs collapsing from snowfall. I was quick enough to tell them that was my other purpose for it, but I didn't think of that until they mentioned it." Bert explained.

Bert, being the clever scientist that he was, would come up with all kinds of inventions and sell them. It was easier than getting a job.

"This one sounds even better than your heated coasters. Congratulations once again." Dennis said. "Thanks, so, how was your trip? Any romance?" Bert asked. "No, nothing yet. I don't know if there is going to be any. I do have something that you might be interested in though. Remember when you had that book about Satanism published?" Dennis asked.

"Yea, that was a long time ago. How did you remember that?" Bert asked. "Well, something I encountered on my trip made me think about it. I think you may be able to help me on this." Dennis said, and he explained everything about the church to him.

Bert listened carefully and he seemed shocked at what he was hearing. "That was a long time ago in my life, but I will help you anyway I can with it." Bert said.

"Thanks, I thought you might be interested in this one, especially since you had such a good time on the last one. Oh, wait, that reminds me. I have something else to tell you about." Dennis said, and then he told Bert all about Amy's boyfriend's death.

"Oh man, I guess it worked." Bert said. "What do you mean by that?" Dennis asked. "Promise me you won't get mad." Bert said. "Oh jeez, what did you do?" Dennis asked, with horror in his voice.

"Well. I decided to have a little fun. Those guys are all pieces of garbage anyway." Bert started to say. "What did you do? Tell me!" Dennis insisted.

"Not if you're going to get mad. Calm down and I'll tell you." Bert said. "Okay, I'm not going to get mad. I am calm. Now tell me!" Dennis demanded. "Well, I kinda, sorta mailed those photos to his address." Bert said, with the sound of fear in his voice.

"I don't believe you! Are you insane? We could get into trouble if they track that back to us!" Dennis yelled. "Relax, what could they do? Besides, they won't track it back to us. I made sure there weren't any finger prints on them and I typed the address on the envelope and I wore gloves throughout my entire project." Bert said, as he let out a small laugh.

"You are one sick bastard. I hope you had fun. I did tell you not to show anyone those pictures. Do you remember that?" Dennis asked. "I'm sorry, I couldn't help myself. C'mon, I'm rich again. I'll take you out tonight and maybe I'll share my big secret with you." Bert offered.

Later that evening Bert, Dennis and Dr. Hynes all went out for dinner to the Bar-Restaurant in the neighborhood. After they ate, they sat at the bar talking and watching the news on the TV in the corner.

After watching a news story about Jin Meir cards, these were trading cards put out by a company in a country off Asia. Kids collected and traded them. It turned out that some kids in a quiet suburb of Boston were on one of the kid's front stoop playing with the cards.

An argument started over which cards belonged to which child. The kids were under the impression that some Jin Meir cards were worth more than others were. All the kids wanted the ones that were supposedly worth more.

The mother of one of the kids came to the front door to find out what all of the arguing was about. A large child began yelling at the woman, telling her that her son stole his Jin Meir cards.

The mother attempted to resolve the issue. The large child started punching her in the face repeatedly. The woman fell to the ground. Her son tried to push the large kid away but he was too big for him to move. When the large kid realized what he had done, he made a run for it back to his house.

"You see? That is why these stupid parents should only buy their kids toys that are made in the USA!" One of the guys at the bar yelled out, as some of the customers laughed.

Bert turned to Dennis and mentioned how he shouldn't waste his time investigating the church. "These Jin Meir cards are really the evil things you should be investigating, and they are getting the children at a young age." He joked, as a reporter came on and announced a story about the worlds first cloned sheep.

"Wait a second! Every one shut up! Put that louder!" Bert yelled, as the bar became silent. The bartender walked over and turned up the volume. The story was about a scientist from Europe who cloned the world's first living creature, a baby sheep.

Bert started to lose it. He slammed his glass down and it shattered on the bar. "That son of a bitch! God dammit!" He cursed and hollered as an employee of the bar held his arms down to his sides. "Dr. Bleckard, are you going to calm down or am I going to have to escort you out?" The man asked.

"Shit! Dammit! I can't believe this! Yes, yes. I'll calm down. I'm sorry." Bert said. Dr. Hynes told the bartender that he would pay for any damages as he pulled Bert to the side with Dennis. They questioned Bert as to what he was up to.

"Do you really want to know? I can't explain unless you take a ride with me to my laboratory." Bert said.

A while later the guys were at Bert's house. Bert brought them into the den and made them a drink. He told them to sit still for a moment. Dr. Hynes and Dennis were very confused and anxious to find out what exactly was going on. They whispered to each other, questioning Bert's sanity.

Bert walked back into the den area. "Well, I told you that I might be sharing my secret with you tonight. Now it is ruined." Bert said, as he opened the door a little wider and he pulled in a white tiger on a leash.

"You sick son of a bitch! Get that thing away from me!" Dennis yelled, as he jumped up onto the back of the couch. "What is this all about Bert?" Dr. Hynes asked.

"I would like you to meet, Whitey Exercitatus. He is the world's first cloned tiger. This was my big surprise for the world to see, but that son of a bitch with the sheep beat me to the introduction of cloned animals. Now it doesn't mean as much as it would have." Bert explained.

"This is unbelievable, but please take Whitey away so that I could put my pounding heart back in my chest." Dennis pleaded.

Bert brought the tiger back inside and he returned to explain to the guys that he had worked on this project for close to twenty-five years. He told them that he was scheduled to make this big announcement in the coming weeks and it has been all that he could think about. Now this other scientist went and took all of Bert's glory away.

Over the next few days, Bert was in a state of depression. The guys couldn't get him to leave his house. During that time, the story about Rick was all over town. The way it happened was, after Rick saw the pictures he went to confront Razer, the guy who was beating Amy. The guys called him Razer because they felt his real name, Raymond, was not a tough enough name for his lifestyle. For that matter, who knows why Rick kept his name?

While asking Razer what was going on in the pictures, an argument ensued. One thing led to another and Rick was shot and killed. Now Razer is wanted for murder and he is hiding out.

Razer is also a friend of the guy named David that was arrested after the McDonald's robbery. It turned out that David was released from jail a couple of days before Rick's death and he was brought back in for questioning regarding the shooting.

Luckily for David a police officer was watching him at the time Rick was murdered and his story checked out. David didn't give any information to the police about Razer.

Razer had contacted David only one time after the shooting, but they didn't have the opportunity to talk very long. Razer was only able to inform him that the shooting was an accident and he let him know where he would be hiding out.

He was at the neighborhood water tower. That was another place they hung out and desecrated every once in a while. His plan was to have David bring him food and supplies so that he wouldn't have to chance leaving the spot, but now that the cops had such a close watch on David, that was not going to be easy.

There were a couple of other guys in their gang that he could have asked for help from, but he didn't have the same kind of trust in them that he had in David.

G. Novitsky

Chapter Eight
"Re-visit the Worshiper's"

After a couple of days had passed, Dennis was in his office checking his messages. He skipped over a couple of them and came to an interesting one. It was from the woman he met at the church parking lot, who wanted to hire him to investigate the church. "Dennis? Hi, it's Tara. I am here with my friend Glenn; he is the organizer of our group. We would like to let you know that we are ready to have you come down and start your work." She said. She also left a number where they could be reached.

Dennis was pretty excited. He was looking forward to getting the investigation underway. Before he returned Tara's call, he decided to give Rosa a call. He dialed the number and he heard a friendly hello from the other end. "Rosa? It's Dennis. How are you?" He asked.

"Oh my God, hi, I am doing good. Everything is great except Amy is still not completely back to normal yet but what is normal for a teenage girl anyway?" Rosa joked. Dennis let out a small laugh. "I just got a message from that group I told you about down there. I wanted to let you know that I will probably be stopping down pretty soon." He explained.

"That is great. I am glad they were serious about it. This will give us a chance to see each other again. Do you know when you'll be here?" She asked.

"I don't have a definite date yet, but I will let you know as soon as I do." He added. "What's new up there? Did they find the guy that killed Rick?" She asked. "From what I hear, they are still looking for him. I haven't heard much." Dennis said.

"Well, if I really cared about him, I would've hired you to look into it, since you are so good at that." She said. "Thanks for the vote of confidence. I have to make a couple more phone calls, so I will give you a ring before I head down there." He said.

"Okay, it was great hearing from you. I look forward to the visit." She said. "Same here. See you soon." Dennis said, as he hung up. "Dennis, I miss you." Rosa said, as she realized she was talking to herself.

Dennis then returned the call to Tara. He spoke to Glenn and they squared away the details. Glenn explained that they arranged a place for Dennis to live during his stay and they agreed on a very satisfying salary for Dennis as long as he gets enough information to have the church closed or at least redirected back into the way it used to be.

Soon after that call, Dennis was able to get in touch with Bert. "You're going to snap out of this depression and take a vacation down south with me." Dennis told him. After some persuading, Bert agreed to take the trip.

They arranged a day that was good for both of them to leave and worked it out so they could be away for a couple of weeks.

When Bert spoke to Dr. Hynes on the phone, he asked him to come along for the trip. Dr. Hynes already had plans to be at his cottage in Maine. "Too bad you're going down there, I could've used your company up at your favorite getaway." Dr. Hynes said.

Bert felt like a wishbone being pulled in two directions. He loved the cottage, but he also had some curiosity about the church. He had to go with Dennis; he already gave his word.

"Set a date for your next trip and I'll be there." Bert said. "We'll set it up when you get back, enjoy your trip." Dr. Hynes said, as he hung up the phone.

Dr. Hynes left for his trip that Friday night. He wanted to wake up there so he could start fishing first thing Saturday morning. When he woke up, he glanced out of the window to the east and caught a beautiful sunrise over the water. He turned to look out of the other window and noticed some construction work going on about fifty yards away from his property.

"I guess this is the end of my seclusion. Now they are all gonna start building around my hidden paradise." He thought to himself.

While he was getting his boat ready for a day of fishing, Dennis and Bert were just arriving at Glenn's office. They didn't expect such a state of the art office for a group that seemed like it didn't have much direction.

The computers, phones, fax machines, copy machines and desks were all rather new. The group only consisted of seven people but the office could hold twenty comfortably.

Glenn walked over and introduced himself. He was a short, stocky, attractive man. He brought Dennis and Bert into the lounge area and offered them a drink. Bert had a sprite and Dennis had a scotch.

Glenn was surprised that Bert came along, but he was happy that he did. Glenn wanted as many people on his side that he could get.

They had a short, informal interview. Dennis told Glenn about his prior cases and informed him that this is the first time he ever worked on anything like this. That is when he explained how Bert is somewhat of an expert on the subject. Glenn was very impressed with Bert's education and background.

Glenn explained how he wanted everything to work and he let them know that any resources they needed would be made available, all they had to do was ask. They spoke for a short while before Glenn showed them where they would be staying. The rooms were just as impressive as the office.

Once they made themselves comfortable, Dennis gave Rosa a call. He informed her that he was in town and if she wanted to get together, he was available. They made plans for later in the week.

Early the following morning Dennis brought Bert to the church so he could get a feeling for what they were up against.

They walked inside and it didn't have the same cold, dreary feeling like Dennis remembered. "This doesn't seem so evil to me." Bert said after looking around. "To tell you the truth, I agree. Maybe when I take you to one of Father Servat's masses you'll get to see what I witnessed the last time I was here." Dennis said. "I am looking forward to it." Bert replied, as they walked around and investigated.

Dennis tossed and turned in his bed all night wondering what happened, why the church seemed so much brighter and cheerier than his last visit. He also figured that if it stayed like that, it would make an easy payday.

The next day, Dennis and Bert attended Father Servat's twelve-noon mass. The church was still in better spirits and even Father Servat seemed like a different person. He was performing the ceremony as an ordinary catholic priest would. The only thing that didn't change were the cold stares on most of the churchgoers faces. There was still something evil about that. Bert also took notice.

They were walking to the parking lot after the mass, Dennis was fumbling through his pocket to get his car keys. "I really don't understand what is going on here, it seems a bit strange. I am going to have a word with this priest. Do you think he knows I am here to check on him?" He asked. "I don't think that could be the case, unless your friends from the group are part of the game that's going on. If you want to speak with him, why don't you find out when he hears Penance? You could talk to him in one of those little boxes." Bert suggested.

"I knew I invited you for a reason, that is a great idea." Dennis said, as he went back in to find out about receiving Penance.

Later that evening, close to six o'clock, Dennis went back to the church to see Father Servat. He entered the confessional. "Father Servat?" He asked. "Yes my son. Could you begin with an Act of Contrition?" Father Servat asked.

I am sorry Father, but I have not been to confession in a long time." Dennis replied. "That's not quite it, but it is close." Father Servat replied. "No Father, I was informing you that I am not really here to confess. I would just like to ask you a few questions." Dennis explained.

"Oh that is different, my son. If that is the case, maybe you would be more comfortable in my office." He replied.

They went to his office in the rectory. Father Servat offered Dennis a seat and a drink. "What do you have? I suppose just wine? Dennis asked, as he let out a small, nervous laugh. "If that's what you prefer? I was thinking more on the lines of coffee." Father Servat said.

"Coffee sounds good. Thank you Father." Dennis said, as he tried to control the nervous feeling he had. Father Servat excused himself for a moment. While he was gone Dennis admired the crucifix behind the desk and the other religious statues. At least they looked religious, just somewhat out of the ordinary.

Father Servat returned and handed Dennis a cup of coffee with sugar packets and a cup of cream on the side. "So, what is on your mind?" Father Servat asked.

"Well, I don't want to sound too forward, Father, but I would like to ask you about your church. I was in town a couple of weeks ago and I stopped in for a mass. I couldn't help but notice that there was something different about your mass as opposed to other ones that I have attended." Dennis explained.

"I will be honest with you. I know that I may say mass somewhat different from other priest's or pastors. I know there are many people who object to my way of spreading the Lord's word. I also know that some of them go so far as to protest against me in the parking lot across the street. That protesting only began a short while ago, and that protesting is what made me realize that I am not pleasing everyone in this town. Since it has been brought to my attention, I have been trying to change slowly. I don't want to scare off any would be churchgoers, like yourself." He explained.

"I did notice that you have changed from the last time I attended your mass, but the people who attend the mass have a strange coldness about them. Where does that come from?" Dennis asked.

"That is another thing that I noticed. I really can't explain that. I think it may have something to do with this town from before I arrived. I am trying to bring them around." Father Servat said.

"I am sorry if I was pushy Father. I was just concerned. I would like to thank you for your time." Dennis said with embarrassment. "It is my pleasure. Come see me anytime. It is good to know there are people here that are interested in what is going on at their parish." He said. Dennis thanked him again and walked out to his car with his head hung low as Father Servat watched him from the window and smiled.

While Dennis was at the church, Bert was at Glenn's office. He spoke with Glenn and Tara for a short while. Afterwards, Dennis and Bert met back at their room. Dennis explained how bad he felt for questioning Father Servat and how nice he was about the whole situation.

"I figured that might be the case." Bert said. "What do you mean by that?" Dennis asked. "Well, I got the impression from your friends at the office that they are up to some kind of game. They have all of this money to throw around, and they are not too thorough in their assumptions of what happens at that church. I get the impression that they are behind something bigger in this town. Maybe you should do your best to prove to them that the church is on the up and up and use their money to start investigating them." Bert suggested.

"I don't know. I have a whole new outlook on this case now. Let's just go out with Rosa and her cousin tomorrow night and have a good time, we'll enjoy all of the good things these people are giving us. I'll clear my head and decide what I should do on Tuesday or Wednesday." Dennis said.

Chapter Nine
"Wonderful First Impression"

June 2003

Monday morning Dr. Hynes was on his way back from his trip to Maine. He stopped along the way at a small diner to get a quick bite to eat. All he could think about was how much it bothered him that after all of the years he had been going to his cottage for seclusion; someone was building so close. He felt that soon enough more people would be breaking ground near his hideaway.

While he was eating, Dr. Hynes overheard a couple at the booth next to his. They were discussing a similar situation to the one that Dennis and Bert were currently looking in to.

The couple mentioned a church in their neighborhood that could possibly be practicing devil worship. This couple was not upset about it though. They sounded more intrigued than anything else.

Dr. Hynes quickly asked the waitress for a pen and a piece of paper. She gave him her ordering pad and he took some notes, as to the name of the church and the street names that the couple mentioned. Dr. Hynes figured that Dennis would be interested in hearing about it.

Later on, back down south, Dennis and Bert were arriving at Linda's house. Amy answered the door. "Hey kiddo, how are you feeling?" Dennis asked. "Oh, it's you." She replied with lack of enthusiasm towards Dennis.

"Yea, it's me, and I would like you to meet my friend Bert." Dennis said. Amy went to shake Bert's hand as she looked at him and became mesmerized. She seemed to have some sort of a crush on him at first glance.

Bert didn't notice her attraction to him, but as soon as she left the room, Dennis was quick to joke about Bert having a little admirer.

"Hi, I'm Rosa, I see you met little miss personality." Rosa said, as she walked in and shook Bert's hand. "I'm Bert, it's nice to meet you Rosa. She seems like a nice girl." Bert replied.

"She is, it's just lately that she has been in sort of a daze, and short tempered. I'm sure it's all related to that boy's death." Rosa stated, as she gave Dennis a hug. "Come in, have a seat, get comfortable. What can I get you to drink Bert? I know it's a scotch for you Dennis." She said.

"I'll have a sprite, if its not too much trouble." Bert said. "Sprite? We're going to loosen up and have a good time. How about a beer?" Rosa suggested. "I was going to start off with a sprite and see if I liked you guys enough to loosen up with." Bert joked. "Oh, we have another comedian with us tonight." Rosa said while laughing.

"Okay, I'll take a beer. I can see I'm going to like you." Bert said. Rosa smiled as she walked out to get the drinks. Dennis picked up the remote control and found a news channel on the television.

A short while later, Rosa returned with Linda and the drinks. She introduced Bert to Linda. The four of them spent the evening in the living room just talking and laughing.

Rosa asked Dennis how the church case was going. He explained to her how they thought there was more to it, and that the people who hired him seemed suspicious. Rosa felt that was a major turn of events.

"Wow, what do you plan on doing now?" She asked. "I'm really not so sure right now. They are acting strange and I also spoke to the priest last night. He is a very nice man, he knows how the neighborhood is portraying him and he is doing his best to change his style to make them happy. Even Bert spoke with the people who hired me and he also feels the same way I do about them. I may even use the money they are paying me to build a case against them." Dennis explained. Rosa found the whole situation very intriguing.

Throughout the evening, Amy popped her head in every so often. It was obvious to Dennis that she just wanted to get a glance of Bert each time. Rosa asked her to join them, but Amy acted as if she was content sitting upstairs on the computer.

"So, you're one of those e-mailers?" Bert joked. "I used to be online a lot more than I have been recently, but I am starting to get back into it." Amy responded, as she headed back upstairs to the computer.

"Don't you just get a kick out of those fools who forward those nonsense chain letters along as if they really think those ridiculous punishments are going to happen?" Dennis asked, as he laughed.

"You are so right. I delete that garbage as soon as I get passed the first line, where it says to forward it to five or ten or however many gullible idiots you know." Linda said.

"Yea, yea, if you don't, your second cousin will get hit by a low flying helicopter and lose his scalp, or your grandmother will get AIDS from a circus gorilla." Dennis said, as everyone let out a laugh.

"And if you do send it, you'll have good luck for the next ten years, and if you act now, you will also see something very special appear on your monitor right after you send the letter. After all of that bull shit, then it says, this really works; my uncle in Bumblehump New Mexico inherited forty-five trillion dollars one hour after he sent it to everyone in his address book." Bert said, as they all tried to catch their breath from laughing so hard.

"Stop me if you heard this one, it said it was a true story. A peanut salesman and a perfume salesman meet in front of a potential customer's house. The peanut salesman is holding a jar of his finest items. The perfume salesman has a donkey on a leash.

The peanut salesman asks what the donkey is for. The perfume salesman says, I spray the perfume on him so that my customers can see that even an animal will smell great with my product.

The peanut salesman thought that was a good sales pitch. He offered the perfume salesman a peanut as he took a whiff of the donkey. The peanut salesman said, damn I love the way your ass smells. The perfume salesman responded, thank you and may I say that your nuts are the finest I ever tasted?" Rosa recalled the joke, as Bert and Dennis laughed.

"That was just awful. Who sent you that one?" Linda asked, as she giggled out loud.

They had a really good time but the next day was back to work for Dennis. He met with Glenn and Tara over lunch. He explained to them that he met with Father Servat and he thinks that he will be able to convince him to straighten up his act. The two of them seemed like they were impressed with Dennis' work so far. They even gave him an advance on the first half of his salary.

Dennis started thinking that it was too easy and these two had to be up to something. He decided to play along and tell them that he should be able to clean the church up all on his own within a week or two. He figured he had nothing to lose since Father Servat planned on changing for the people in the town anyway.

Over the next few days everything seemed to be going smooth, almost too smooth, Dennis felt. The complaints about the church had stopped and the appearance became less dreary. The churchgoers still had that possessed look about them, Dennis figured that was from living in that little town so long. He joked to Rosa that he should get out of there before he had that look also.

He met with Rosa a few more times before he and Bert wrapped up all of their business. Dennis left it as, they would stay in touch over the phone and visit whenever he or she was able to.

Bert gave Dennis a hard time on the trip back about him not making his move. "I don't know if she feels like that about me, we became too friendly. I think it's too late to turn it into anything else." Dennis explained.

"Come on, it's never too late, you're just afraid." Bert commented. "What about that little admirer of yours?" Dennis asked, to change the subject. "I didn't see whatever it was that you were imagining." Bert said.

"Oh, give me a break, that girl couldn't take her eyes off of you. The younger ones always had a thing for you." Dennis said. Bert laughed. "Well, that's true. Only the naive ones show an interest in me." He joked.

"They may be up to something, but they make good on their payments." Dennis said, as he counted the cash that Glenn and Tara gave him.

"No legitimate business would hand you all of that money to just have a few words with a priest, they are up to something. You better be careful. How did you leave it with them anyway?" Bert asked.

"They gave me half for now. They said if everything stays the way it is, I will get the other half in a month. If it goes back to the way it was I will have to do some real investigative work. Seems fair to me." Dennis said.

"A month, huh, that's not a bad deal. I guess this trip was worth it." Bert said, as Dennis handed him his percentage.

They arrived back in town later that afternoon. The first stop was Dennis' office. Bert threw his jacket over a chair as he walked in. Dennis hit the play button on his answering machine. He talked over a couple of the less interesting messages, and then there was one from Dr. Hynes.

"Hey, Dennis, it's me. I don't know when you guys are returning from your trip, but I came across something interesting on my way back from Maine. Let me just say that the town you went to is not the only one with devil worshipers. Call me back when you get time." Dr. Hynes' recording said.

Dennis and Bert looked at each other in surprise. "I don't know if I want to hear about this one." Bert said. "Me neither, but he got me curious. Should I call him back now?" Dennis asked. "I was just going to ask you why you haven't dialed yet." Bert joked.

Dennis called him back and put him on the speakerphone. Dr. Hynes explained the whole situation about the couple in the diner and how they were talking about another church that sounded like the one they were already investigating.

"If you like, I know the area and I have the name of the church. It's St. Ezra's. I could take a ride with you." Dr. Hynes suggested. "Why don't we do it when we decide to make a run up to your cottage?" Bert hinted. "How did I know you would work a visit to the cottage into this?" Dr. Hynes joked.

"Make sure your boat is ready for a day on the waves." Bert said, as he cracked a laugh. "That reminds me, you are going to have to make a visit soon. Soon enough, it's not going to be as peaceful as you remember it. I noticed some construction going on outside of my property. There goes the neighborhood." Dr. Hynes said.

"Are you serious? Man, a good thing never lasts too long. Is there anyway we could put a stop to it?" Bert asked. "I doubt that. It's a free country, if people want to move in next door, who am I to stop them? Maybe it won't be so bad. It's possible that it may be a quiet older couple or something. My only concern is that the building may spark an outbreak of other people wanting to build in the area." Dr. Hynes explained.

They went on with their plans and decided to take a trip up there over the weekend.

G. Novitsky

Chapter Ten
"A Second Church"

July 2003

They decided to head up to Maine on Friday night. Dennis did his research over the week to find out exactly where the church was. They took a look at it that night while passing through the small town. They didn't plan on going in until Sunday mass.

From the outside it looked just as eerie as St. Barabus' did the first time Dennis saw it. "Wow, that couple was right. This place looks like the outside of hell. How does a community let this happen?" Dr. Hynes asked, as they stared at the dark, gloomy building behind the trees. Even the cross on top seemed run down and ready to collapse.

"Maybe this is the neighborhood children's Halloween entertainment. I wouldn't be surprised if there is another Tara hanging around looking for someone like you Dennis." Bert said. "I don't know what in the world Glenn and Tara are up to, but this does look very similar to the other one." Dennis said.

"Let's get moving. This place is giving me the creeps in the dark. We'll come back Sunday morning, when it's light outside." Dr. Hynes suggested. He sounded like a frightened child.

They continued their trip and woke up early Saturday morning to get a full day in at sea. Dr. Hynes came walking into the living room where Bert was already up, having a cup of coffee. "So, where is all this construction that you're so worried about?" Bert asked.

"It was right over there." Dr. Hynes said, as he held his robe closed with one hand and with the other, he pointed in the direction where the builders were the week before. "I don't see anything. It must have been your imagination." Bert joked.

"I don't get it. It's gone. I don't know what happened but now I am happy about my place again." Dr. Hynes said excitedly. "See what happens when you wish hard enough? Now get yourself in gear, it's time to get on the water." Bert said.

They set sail and went out a couple of miles off shore. Dr. Hynes set up his fishing gear, as the waves became a bit rough. Dennis started to get a little nervous as the boat rocked and swayed under a clear blue sky. "Sit down, have a drink. Are you gonna let some waves startle you?" Dr. Hynes asked, as he let out a laugh.

"Do we have life jackets on this thing?" Dennis asked. "No, you were supposed to bring your own." Dr. Hynes joked. "How far is the coast guard? Do you have any seamen on hand?" Dennis asked. "If you do, I suggest you wash it off." Bert chimed in and the three of them laughed out loud.

"You sure know what to say to loosen up a situation." Dennis said, as he grabbed a beer and sat down. He started to get used to the swaying and he was eventually able to enjoy the ride.

They fished, joked and discussed their upcoming visit to the church until the sun went down.

The next morning after Dr. Hynes organized everything around the cottage; they were off to the church. They arrived just as the ten o'clock mass was beginning.

Even in the daylight, the church appeared darker and more disturbing than St. Barabus' did for Dennis' first visit. The people of this church also had the same cold stares as the other ones.

They stayed for the beginning of the mass and listened to the priest. He seemed to have a normal approach to saying a mass. The thing that got Dennis' attention was how the people would refer to God as, Domi. He didn't quite understand that.

The three of them started to feel uncomfortable about twenty minutes in. It felt as if everyone was watching them. Not only did the people have those disturbing stares but Dennis also thought that they were being watched because, it's not every Sunday that you see three grown men standing in church together.

He motioned to Bert and Dr. Hynes that it was time to get out of there as he tucked one of the mass books into his jacket.

None of them said a word until they got into the car. "How uncomfortable was that?" Dr. Hynes questioned. "Thank God you suggested leaving." Bert said. No, thank Domi." Dennis joked. "Yea, what was that about? When did they re-name God?" Dr. Hynes asked.

"Ah, you know they give him hundreds of different names, Lord, Yahweh, Messiah. The list goes on. I wouldn't make such a big deal about that." Bert explained. "I guess you're right. We should really be worrying about who is behind this and if it is connected to the St. Barabus situation." Dennis suggested.

Dennis considered the possibility of the two church's having some kind of a connection as he found himself up all night at his office reading passages from the mass book that he brought home from the church.

He felt guilty about taking something from the church but he convinced himself that he did it for the sake of something greater. He highlighted several passages that caught his attention, such as:

1.   Thus the heavens and the earth were completed in all their vast array.

By the seventh day Domi had finished the work he had been doing.

So on the seventh day he rested from all his work.

Domi blessed the seventh day and made it a day for him to be worshiped.

Because on it, he rested from all the work of creating that he had done.

The worshipers should acknowledge his creations.

2. Seven days passed after Domi struck the river.

Then Domi said to Proteg, Go to Pharaoh and say to him,

"This is what Domi says, let my people go, so that they may worship me.

If you refuse to let them go, I will plague your whole country.

3. The angel of Domi went up from his first land to his new land and said, "I brought you up out of the old land and led you into the land that I swore to give to your forefathers. I will never break my covenant with you and you shall not make a covenant with the people of this land.

But you shall break down their altars.

Although he was not a very religious man, he knew that these passages had to have been from the actual bible and transformed into a way to give them an alternate meaning.

He didn't share these findings with Bert or Dr. Hynes just yet. He wanted to bring more puzzle pieces together before getting the guys involved any further.

On the other side of town, Razer, the gang member who killed Amy's boyfriend, was on his cell phone speaking with Amy. He explained to her that he really didn't want to kill him. He swore it was an accident.

"How did you guys get into such a horrible fight anyway?" Amy asked. "That is what I wanted to talk to you about. Something very strange happened. I came home a few nights ago and he stopped over. We talked for a short while and then he questioned what I was doing with you. I knew he was gonna find out about us sooner or later but not the way he did.

He opened up an envelope and he had pictures taken of you and me from the last time we were together. He said someone mailed them to him without a return address. Before I could say a word, he started throwing punches at me. I tried to fight him off and calm him down but he was in a rage.

I was able to pull out my gun from the cabinet. I only wanted to scare him with it to make him stop. That only made him angrier. He came at me like a maniac and that's when the gun went off by accident and killed him." Razer said, as he started to become emotional.

"I think I know who may have given him those pictures. My mother thinks I don't know that she hired an investigator to watch Rick and me but I figured it out after this guy Dennis started hanging around with her. He must have been the one who took those pictures. He probably thought that you were Rick." Amy suggested.

"Man, that's messed up. Why would he want to give Rick the pictures though?" Razer asked. "I don't know, maybe he is just a screwed up person. He has been spending too much time around my mother as it is, now it looks like he is playing games with me and my friends. Should I tell my mother?" Amy questioned.

"No, don't say anything to her yet. Do you think you can find out how I can get my hands on this guy?" Razer asked.

"I will go through my mother's things and see what I can find. I'll call you back after that." She said, and they hung up.

Before Rosa and Linda came down the stairs, Amy fished through her mother's pocket book. She went into her wallet where all of her credit and business cards were and she came across Dennis' card. She wrote down the address and phone number and put the card back in the slot where she found it.

Dennis was in his office searching the Internet for any information related to Domi, or any kind of mysterious worship. After an hour or so of looking, he was shocked to find a recent news article about a church in Wyoming that was practicing the same type of religion as the other two churches he visited.

He printed the article and sent an e-mail to the author. He questioned the author as to how he could obtain more information regarding the church and if there were any other similar cases reported. He also sent the three passages from the mass book and asked if there was any significant meaning to them.

He called Bert a short while later to inform him of what he came across. He still didn't want to involve the guys in his mission but he felt he needed to share this. "You don't quit, do you? Do you think your friends from down south have anything to do with this one too?" Bert asked.

"I may be able to find out soon enough. The month is almost up and they should be calling within the next few days. Why don't you seem too interested in all of this? I figured you, of all people would be excited by this type of thing." Dennis inquired.

"I'm sorry, I have things on my mind and I'm still bothered by that sheep incident. When you need my help on this thing, I promise I'll be there for you." Bert said comfortingly.

"That's better, I hope you snap out of this depression soon. I really want you to be there when I put this whole thing together, and I know I will eventually." Dennis said with confidence.

"I know you will too. I have an idea, I know I'm not a big party animal but maybe a good night out, getting a load on will get me out of the way I'm feeling. Are you up for it?" Bert asked.

"Sounds good to me. Should I come pick you up?" Dennis asked. "No, not tonight. I'm finishing up writing what I am going to say tomorrow night, when I tell all of those people that my big secret was ruined by someone who beat me to it. I figure after tomorrow, my big problem will be off my back and we could go out afterwards." Bert suggested.

"It's a plan. Do you want me to go to the meeting with you?" Dennis asked. "No, this is not a celebration. You can meet me at the restaurant down the block from the hall, where we went last time. If I don't talk to you before then, just meet me there at around seven o'clock and put your drinking shoes on." Bert said. "Okay, I'll see you there." Dennis replied, and they hung up.

Chapter Eleven
"Another Round for my Friend"

The next evening, Dennis arrived at the restaurant at seven o'clock, like Bert asked him to. He sat at the bar and looked up toward the television in the corner. Most of the tables on the restaurant side were taken, but only a few people were sitting at the bar for drinks. "How's it going? Are you Dennis?" The bartender asked.

"Yes, yes I am." Dennis replied in a surprised tone. "Dr. Bleckard called, he said that he will be running a little late. He said to make yourself comfortable and this first scotch here is on him." The bartender said, as he slid the glass in front of Dennis. "Oh, okay then. Thanks, cheers." Dennis said, as he raised the glass and smiled.

By the time Bert walked in it was close to nine o'clock. Dennis already had almost five drinks and he was starting to feel them. "Sorry buddy, it went longer than I expected. Did you get my message?" Bert asked.

"Yes, I did. Don't worry about it, I was enjoying myself here. Now it's time for you to catch up." Dennis said, as he ordered another scotch for himself and a scotch and a shot of whiskey for Bert.

"That's very nice of you but, I'm not doing a shot by myself. Make that two shots of whiskey!" Bert yelled to the bartender. "So, was it painful back at the hall?" Dennis asked. Bert explained that it wasn't as bad as he anticipated.

At the hall he told the crowd that he had something big planned for the evening but the sheep that was introduced recently, put a damper on things. After he thanked the crowd for their interest in his work and his few minutes of jokes, he decided to bring out Whitey.

Bert managed to amaze the crowd after all of his doubt. Although the first cloned animal was already introduced to the world, there was something more impressive about a white tiger over a sheep. Bert left the hall feeling better about himself than he thought he would.

"See that? The worse you expect something to be, the better it turns out." Dennis said while slurring. The guys sat there and drank until close to midnight before Bert suggested they take a walk down the block to catch a taxi. Neither one of them was in any shape to drive.

They said goodnight to the bartender and then stumbled out into the cool breeze. Dennis was slightly wobblier than Bert was. He joked about how the town was spinning as they walked down the sidewalk. Dennis was laughing as he bumped into a man coming from the opposite direction.

"Watch where you're walking, asshole!" The man angrily said. "Give it a break, pal! My friend had too much to drink!" Bert yelled back. "Yea, screw off!" Dennis said while trying to gain his balance. "You drunken idiot!" The man said, as he continued on his way.

Dennis and Bert were still laughing as they stumbled along. All of a sudden, Dennis was struck in the back of the head with a bottle. The man quietly attacked him from behind with it.

Dennis fell to the ground. Bert started to run after the man but he knew he wouldn't be able to catch him, besides, he had to make sure that Dennis was okay.

Dennis was lying in a puddle of his own blood when Bert rushed to him, he took his jacket off and wrapped it around Dennis' head to stop the bleeding. He picked him up and put him in a taxi. The driver wanted to take them directly to the hospital until Bert explained that he was a doctor and it would be quicker to get Dennis to his lab where he could stitch it up himself. The driver was convinced that was better than waiting in a line at the hospital.

Bert spent several hours working on the wound. He made sure all of the glass was out and he double-checked Dennis' blood count before he had him looking as good as new.

Bert was completely exhausted by the end of the procedure. He carried Dennis to his bed and he took the couch. Both of them slept until after three the next day. Dennis woke up holding his bandaged head. "What the hell is this?" He asked himself, as he started to get up to find out where he was.

"Good morning. You must have one hell of a hang over!" Bert yelled from the kitchen. He served up a late lunch and explained the bandage to Dennis as they ate.

"I guess your big night on the town wasn't what we were expecting." Dennis said. "Uh, it could have been worse. Be thankful that you're alive." Bert said. "I guess you're right about that. Is all of the glass out of my head?" Dennis asked. "No, I figured I would leave some in there for a memory. Of course it's all out.

Don't question my surgical skills, I made a tiger on my own, remember?" Bert joked.

They laid around for a while before they got the strength to lift themselves up and get into the car. Eventually Bert drove Dennis to his office.

The office was in shambles when they arrived. The door was off of the hinges. The desk was turned over on its side with all of the computer parts; telephone, TV and equipment scattered around. There was a note taped to the window. "Mind your business Mr. investigator. This is just the beginning of what can happen to you. We know where you are at all times." It said.

"Dammit! Sons of bitch's!" Dennis growled, as he punched the wall. He could only expect that this was some how related to the bottle incident. Bert tried to calm him down as he glanced around in utter disbelief of the way the office appeared.

The two of them cleaned up as best they could, most of the electronic items that were thrown around were still in functioning condition. "Will you help me lug this stuff over to my house?" Dennis asked with a pathetic, sad look in his eyes, under his bandage.

They managed to bring everything over to Dennis' house and pick up his car from the bar in less than four hours. By the time midnight had arrived, Bert was on his way back home and Dennis was lying on his couch exhausted. He gathered the strength to pick up the phone and dial Rosa's number. She answered the phone and he let her know it was him. "Oh my God! Is everything all right? You sound awful." Rosa said.

He told her about the bottle and the break in, and he apologized for calling so late. "Oh, don't be silly.

You know I'm usually up late. What are you going to do about this?" She asked. "I have a few different ideas, but I'm not going to make any decisions until my brain stops hurting." He joked.

Dennis felt comfortable discussing the situation with Rosa. She seemed like a true friend. He explained that one of his choices would be to leave the New England area and continue his cases from somewhere else. He also considered working from his house and setting his office up in a way to capture whoever was responsible for the break in.

After Rosa heard all about it, she wanted these people caught too. She also felt that the guy who hit him with the bottle was responsible for the damage in the office.

Dennis told Rosa that he really missed her and he would like to go down to see her as soon as he is finished reorganizing himself at home. She was extremely happy to hear that and she informed Dennis that it couldn't be soon enough.

G. Novitsky

Chapter Twelve
"Healing the wounds"

August 2003

A couple of painful days for Dennis had passed. He was down to a smaller bandage and his office was now in a small corner of his house. It had been a while since he was able to check his e-mails; he came to a response from Brett, the author of the Internet article about the church in Wyoming.

"Thank you for your recent inquiry regarding my article. In reference to your question about Domi and strange church related activities, I have included six additional articles that I released recently on the subject." The response stated.

All six articles were basically the same story about six different churches. They were spread out through the United States. Besides the one in Wyoming, there were others in Georgia, Arkansas, Iowa, Oklahoma and Brett's home state of Kentucky. He also had an article written about St. Barabus in South Carolina.

Brett also noted that all of the churches had been renamed and most of the new names were not actual Saints. He also included an explanation of the three passages, he mentioned that the first one sounded very much like Genesis 1:29 part 2, The Beginning. The second one he related to Exodus 8:9 part 8, The Plague of Frogs, and the third one he said sounded like Judges 2:4 part 2, The Angel of the Lord at Bokim.

"Write back if you need any further information, or if you think I am missing anything. I hope your questions have been answered. Thank you, Brett Black." The e-mail said in closing.

Dennis typed his response. "Hello again Mr. Black. You have been a great source of information. I was able to visit St. Barabus not too long ago. I sat with the Pastor and discussed how his church was being portrayed to the outside. He seemed like he was doing his best to change the way things were being run. I also met with an organization down there who were trying to put a stop to the evilness they felt the church was giving off. Do you know anything about the organization? I also recently visited another place in Rhode Island, St. Ezra. It appeared to relate to St. Barabus and the other five you wrote about. I look forward to hearing back from you again. Thank you, Dennis." He wrote and he gave his phone number so Brett would be able to get in touch.

Back in South Carolina, Rosa was discussing what happened to Dennis with Linda over dinner while Amy listened in. Rosa told them how upset the whole thing made her and how she would like to help Dennis work his way through it. Linda was supportive toward Rosa but Amy gave a look as if Dennis deserved what happened.

"What is with you, young lady?" Rosa asked. "Never mind, I just don't care much for that guy." Amy replied. "Why would you say that? He has been nice to you." Rosa inquired. "If you really want to know, I think he had something to do with Rick's death." Amy stated.

"Where did you get that from?" Rosa questioned. "I know he was watching me before we moved down here and I know he took pictures of my friends and me.

I also know that those pictures are the reason Rick was killed." Amy said.

Rosa was silenced. She didn't have any proof of that being false. "That's what I thought." Amy said, as she walked out of the kitchen. "Is that true?" Linda asked. "I really don't know. I am going to have to talk it over with Dennis when he is feeling better. I hope it's not true." She said.

"Do you think Amy knows something about what happened to Dennis?" Linda asked. "I don't know if she knows about it, but if what she is saying about those pictures is true, then I can only assume that her friends are responsible for what happened to him. What am I going to do?" Rosa questioned, as she placed her hands over her face.

"If you want, I can try to talk to her about it." Linda suggested. "I guess anything is worth a shot. Let me know what you find out from her." Rosa said.

Later on that night Linda had a long conversation with Amy about her old friends and the murder of her ex-boyfriend. Amy told Linda about the fight that led up to the murder and how she feels the whole thing is Dennis' fault.

Linda tried to convince her to keep an open mind about Dennis. She explained that Rosa was a close friend of his and she needs a friendship like that.

Amy was not overly pleased to hear that, she just nodded politely so not to start an argument. Once Linda felt like they connected, she gave Amy a kiss good night and shut the light as she walked out of the room.

Amy just thought to herself that her mother should try to be friendlier with her daughter before she looks outside for friends. She thought about heading back to the old gang as she started to fall asleep.

The next day, Dennis received a phone call from Brett Black. Brett filled Dennis in on all of the details about the churches he had written about in his e-mail. He also told Dennis that he knew of the organization that hired Dennis.

Brett didn't hear anything about them being crooked. He only knew of them as being an organization that tried to do what was best for their community and other communities. He said that he would try to find out more about them.

Dennis told him about the church on Rhode Island and the mass book that he took home with him. He read one of the passages over the phone.

"Go and tell my servants, This is what Domi says. You are not the one to build me a house to dwell in. I have not dwelt in a house from the day I brought the old land to the new. I have moved from one site to another, from one dwelling place to another. Wherever I have moved with my followers, did I ever say to any whom I commanded, Why have you not built me a house of cedar. Domi shall be followed to what dwelling he sees fit. Domi must be your priority. Wrath and discomfort will come to those who deny Domi." Dennis read.

"I believe that was taken from the bible and re-worded. It sounds like the book of Chronicles 17:3 with an eerie twist to it, a severely evil twist." Brett said. Brett was a very religious man. Dennis found that to be quite a plus for the case.

They spoke for about an hour and a half. They both thought that they could benefit from one another.

Back in South Carolina, Amy was on the Internet trying to figure out where she could get a cheap plane ticket back to New England. She was fed up with living down south under conditions she was unhappy with. She wanted to stay in touch with Razer but she feared her mother catching her on the phone with him.

Amy was debating calling him to talk about what happened to Dennis, as her mother called her down to eat. She thought to herself how close she was to being caught on the phone with him and leaving would probably be her best option.

Amy went down to eat and tried to keep the conversation friendly. Rosa asked her about her new friends and attempted to reassure her that she was there for any help she needed or if she just wanted to talk. Amy thanked her and said she would keep that in mind as she excused herself and went outside for some air. It was late afternoon but the sun was still shining bright.

Rosa decided to give Dennis a call. He picked up on the second ring with a friendly hello. "Hi Dennis, it's me." Rosa said. "Hey Rosa, I was just thinking about you. Are you okay? Your voice doesn't sound right." Dennis asked.

"Well, not exactly. I guess I should just get it out in the open. I have to ask you something. Do you have a couple of minutes, or is it a bad time?" She asked. "I can talk. I hope there isn't a problem." He answered.

"It's about Amy and her friends. She has been becoming sort of distant towards me and I think it is because of you and I being friendly. She thinks that you had something to do with Rick's death. Did the pictures that you took have anything to do with that?" Rosa asked.

Dennis paused for a moment. "I did want to tell you something about those pictures but I was hoping I wouldn't have to. Those kids did get their hands on some of the pictures and I do believe they caused the fight that lead to the shooting." Dennis explained.

"How could you let them see those pictures? What were you thinking?" She asked. "It really wasn't my fault. I did have someone working with me and he became very careless. By the time it happened, there wasn't a thing I could do to stop it." Dennis said.

"Dennis, I really don't know what to say, except that I am very disappointed in the entire situation. I don't know how you could have let this happen." Rosa said with anger in her voice.

"Look Rosa, I am very sorry that it happened but there is nothing I can do to change it." Dennis explained. "Let me just tell you that I think the reason you took a bottle over the head and your office was ransacked is because of those pictures." She said.

"What makes you think that? Did someone say that?" Dennis asked. "Amy heard some things from her old friends. The whole thing just makes me so worried. I am just so happy that I brought her here away from that danger. I refuse to let her stay in contact with those criminals." Rosa explained.

"Now I guess I know where to begin looking for the people who did this to me." Dennis said. "I guess. Listen Dennis; I don't know if it's such a good idea for you to visit here too soon. It is a very touchy time for Amy and me. Maybe I'll give you a call another time." Rosa said, as she hung up the phone.

"Real great! This is bullshit! Thanks a lot Bert!" Dennis yelled to himself, as he slammed the phone down repeatedly. He felt that Bert's little stunt with the pictures ruined his friendship and any future between Rosa and him.

While his anger was still burning, he decided to give Bert a call. He got the machine, as usual. "Thanks Bert! Thanks a lot! You screwed things up real good for me now!" He started to vent onto the tape as Bert picked up. "What the hell are you yelling about, maniac?" Bert asked.

"Thanks to you and those pictures a kid is dead and now Rosa wants nothing to do with me. Why do you do such stupid things?" Dennis asked. "Are you sure you want to talk to me like this? I could say some things to you also. We don't have to go down this road." Bert warned him.

"About me? What the hell could you say about me? You are way out of line, Mr. bullshit scientist!" Dennis angrily said. "Let's not forget who saved your pathetic life recently. Maybe I should have let you bleed to death on the street, asshole!" Bert said, as he started to boil.

"I wouldn't have been on that damn street if I wasn't going there to console your sorry ass!" Dennis shouted back. "You know what? You're not worth getting myself riled up over. Everything would have ended very nicely if you minded your own damn business, or if you were a real investigator who could have solved the first case I seen you mishandle!" Bert hollered, as he slammed the phone down.

"What the hell does that mean? What is that dumb son of a bitch talking about?" Dennis said to himself, as he tried redialing Bert's number only to hear a busy signal. "Who the hell needs him? And who needs her? Two stupid asses! Screw em! Screw the both of em!" Dennis yelled to himself, as he threw his jacket over his shoulder and headed out toward the corner bar to calm himself down with a scotch or two.

After walking a couple of blocks in the rain, he sat at the bar for close to three hours. He knew the bartender and some of the people at the bar. They made some small talk, but Dennis was more interested in the thoughts going through his own head.

Even though he was extremely angry with both of them, he was hoping to receive messages from Bert and Rosa on his answering machine when he got home. He also considered leaving his profession as an investigator and wondered why Bert said all of those hurtful things about him. He also thought about taking a walk by the apartment building where Amy used to live to see if he could find out anything new about the guy who whacked him with the bottle.

When he finally worked up the courage, that is exactly where he went. The building was only a couple of miles away, so he called a cab to drop him off in the vicinity.

He walked passed the building twice before the door opened and one of the gangsters walked out. Dennis began to walk a bit faster incase the guy recognized him.

"Hey! Hey!" A voice yelled out from behind, as Dennis slowly turned around. "Yea, I'm talkin to you. You got a match?" The kid asked. Dennis fumbled through his pockets nervously hoping to find a book of matches to please the kid.

He grabbed on to something in his inside jacket pocket and pulled it out. To his relief it was a book of matches from the bar. He handed them over to the kid.

"Thanks bro." The kid said, as he lit his cigarette and then offered Dennis the matches back. "No man, it's cool, You keep em." Dennis said. "Good lookin out bro." The kid said, as he turned around and walked in the opposite direction.

"No man, it's cool. You keep em? What the hell was I talking about?" Dennis mocked himself, as he hurried off. That is when he realized, if he was going to get back at these guys, going into their territory by himself was not the way to go about it.

G. Novitsky

Chapter Thirteen
"Focus on the map"

The next day Dennis figured he had to find out a way to nail these gangsters before they nail him, but more importantly, he felt he should start putting together the puzzle that the churches created.

He was pretty surprised that neither Bert nor Rosa attempted to make any contact with him since their arguments, but he figured he would try to put that behind him.

He decided to take into account all of the leads he had on the case so far and start a scrap book. He printed out a map of the United States and marked all of the places that were said to have any kind of strange religious activities going on.

So far he had South Carolina, Rhode Island, Wyoming, Georgia, Arkansas, Iowa, Oklahoma, and Brett's home state of Kentucky. He wrote notes next to each state explaining what he knew about them. South Carolina had the most notes. He also made notations in the mass book as to which passages were the most significant.

He spent the whole day and night working on the project. Before he realized, it was close to midnight and he fell asleep dreaming of the project and the churches.

At around the same time Dennis was nodding off, Amy found a place on the Internet where she could get a flight back to New England for under fifty dollars. The only problem was a credit card. Daringly, she decided to use her mother's card since she didn't have one of her own. She figured that by the time the bill came, she would already be in New England.

It took her a couple of minutes to click on the button to complete the transaction. Quite nervous and a bit shaky, knowing deep down inside what she was doing was wrong; she finally worked up the nerve to click it. "Whew, see that, nothing to it." She said to convince herself that it was okay, as she wiped her forehead with her wrist.

The total, with two-day delivery, came to sixty-two dollars and seventy nine cents. She took sixty-three dollars in cash from her drawer and stashed it under her alarm clock so she could tell her mother to take it once she makes it to New England.

The flight was scheduled to leave Saturday at ten AM. All that was left was getting out of the house without getting caught.

Dennis woke up early the next morning; anxious to speak with Brett about the research he started. He gave Brett a call and they made arrangements to meet and work together on the mysteries of the churches. They planned to get together on Thursday down in Kentucky at Brett's house.

Dennis spent the rest of the day packing and locking up his belongings at home in case of another break in. He called the local police to let them know he would be away for a while. He asked them to pay special attention to his house due to his recent attacks. The police were happy to help him out.

Dennis arrived at Louisville International Airport in Kentucky early Thursday morning. He looked around for the airport cafeteria that Brett described. After a few minutes of looking around and exchanging smiles with friendly people at the airport, one of them guided him to the cafeteria.

"Dennis?" A voice called out. Dennis looked around and noticed a tall thin man by the coffee shop standing next to a table and waving.

"Brett?" Dennis questioned, as he made his way over. They shook hands and Brett offered Dennis a coffee. "Yea, what the heck, set one up for me. I can use one after that flight." Dennis said. He really wanted a scotch but he knew what a religious man Brett was, so he figured he would save that side for when they get to know each other a little better. That is the same reason he tried to curb his language.

They sat there for a little while getting aquatinted. Brett owned and managed a bookstore in the city. He pretty much made his own hours, so he was available to run around with Dennis looking for answers to their questions.

Brett had been married for nine years; he was in his mid thirties. He and his wife were sort of separated and it had all to do with their neighborhood church that suddenly changed.

Brett introduced his wife to that church before they got married. They went together every Sunday. Over the last year or so, when the church began to change, Brett found himself trying to get further away from it as his wife fell deeper into it.

The church became the downfall of their happy marriage. Brett tried his hardest to convince his wife that there was something evil going on there. He gave his best effort to save their marriage but the problems kept getting worse. That is what gave Brett the push to start learning about this new religion and writing about it.

Dennis was moved by Brett's situation. It made him think about his own issues. He told Brett all about Bert, Rosa, Amy and the gang of kids that were after him. Brett was surprised by all of the things that had been going on in Dennis' life.

Brett brought Dennis to his house. He insisted that Dennis stay there for as long as he was in town. After all, his wife was staying with some of her church friends and that left plenty of room around the house.

Dennis showed him the scrapbook and information he had been working on. He was impressed by the amount of material Dennis put together and Brett brought out plenty of other documentation to sort through.

For most of the day and into the evening, they went over all of the information and Brett planned to show Dennis the church in the morning.

The next day, before they went to the church, Dennis decided to check his phone messages. He was still hoping to hear an apology from Bert or Rosa, or both. Instead he came across a frantic message from Tara about St. Barabus. "Dennis, we were going to call you this week and thank you for such a great job but I'm sorry, things went back to the way they were at the church, maybe even worse. I tried talking to the police again but you know how that goes. They aren't doing anything illegal, is what they tell me. Please call me back as soon as you can." The message said. She also left her phone number.

Dennis played the message a second time for Brett. "Wow, she sounds the way I first felt when I couldn't get my wife away from this church. I guess we have our work cut out for us." Brett said.

Dennis wasn't ready to call her back and Brett thought it would be better to wait until after he sees his church.

A short while later, they pulled up in front of the church. "Now this looks like St. Barabus before it calmed down." Dennis said. The church was as disturbing as the one in Rhode Island from the outside, dreary, dark and cold. "I have to take a look inside." Dennis said. "Yes, you should. I would go with you but my wife may be in there and I would rather not stir up any trouble." Brett said.

Dennis walked in slowly. He felt as if he was walking into the other two churches all over again. The same eeriness and the same cold stares were upon him. He even noticed the same smell.

There wasn't a mass underway but some worshipers were standing by the candles and others kneeling by the seats.

Dennis walked slowly to a seat in the back row. He knelt down and pretended to pray. He may have been praying to get out of there safely. When no one was looking, he placed a prayer book into his jacket pocket. He wanted to compare it to the one he took previously.

He remained kneeling for a few moments until he felt he completed a normal prayer session. When he stood up, he wasn't sure if he should make the sign of the cross, or if there was some other ritual that should be made at this church.

He headed to the door without turning his head in either direction. He finally reached the parking lot. "Excuse me sir, you dropped your book." A voice called from behind. Dennis turned around to see a young man standing a few feet away holding the mass book.

"Well, thank you. I don't know what I would have done if I lost this." Dennis said. "You visiting that crazy church?" The man asked. "Yes, yes I was. What do you know about it?" Dennis inquired.

"I don't know too much about it except since that Father Praec started running things, it became a strange little church. That's the least of the strange things I have seen lately though." The man said, as he introduced himself as Darren Harston.

Darren grew up pretty close by, he told Dennis what he knew about the church and he also informed him of some strange incidents that have gone on in his own life since he lost his father.

Dennis was finally able to get away from Darren and he made it safely to the car where Brett was waiting. "What was that all about?" Brett asked. "Oh that guy has issues. Just a bunch of talk about fog and strange roads he has been driving on lately. Even he said there is something wrong with this church." Dennis explained.

"Was it like you expected?" Brett asked. "Worse, just drive away so we can talk." Dennis replied. Once they were a block or two away, Dennis pulled the book out from his jacket and started thumbing through it. "Just as I thought. This is identical to the one I took from Rhode Island." He said.

"I would scold you for stealing from the church, if I considered that brainwashing building a church." Brett said.

"We have to take our act on the road. We have to visit a few more of the places you wrote about and get details and see if they all have the same books. This thing is spread all over, we have to be the ones to put an end to it." Dennis went on. "I have to say, you're right. I think we are in for a long haul." Brett answered.

When they got back to the house, Dennis called Tara immediately. Glenn picked up the phone and put Dennis on the speaker so he and Tara could both hear.

Dennis explained to them what he had just seen in Kentucky and they explained what was going on back in South Carolina. Both places sounded like one in the same. Dennis didn't give all of the details because he was still somewhat skeptical of Glenn and Tara.

Glenn informed Dennis that he was aware of two other churches, the one in Georgia and the one in Arkansas but he had no idea about the one in Kentucky. He explained that the one in Arkansas became known to them only a short while after the one in their own state of South Carolina.

Some of the families around the church in Arkansas helped find their community awareness program, due to a missing boy. It turned out that a young altar boy was reported missing once the strange events started taking place.

The boy's parents started a program down there and all of the communities donated and wanted to help any way they could. Once it was known that the same type of thing was going on down in South Carolina, some residents decided to get a start on protecting the area and the children. That is when Glenn and Tara put together the organization in their spare time.

They were able to make St. Barabus free of altar boys but that was just the beginning of what needed to be done. They were not able to get much help from the local police. They were told, for every complaint, there was also a compliment regarding the church and that the police would just file a report on record. That is around the same time they met Dennis.

The altar boy was later found in the basement of the church hiding. He never spoke out about why he was hiding, everyone just knew that the church became too evil for him to handle.

"Now that this thing seems to be growing, I would really like you to expand on what you are doing about it. We would still like to pay you the rest of the money that we discussed. You may need a team though." Glenn explained.

Dennis was taken back a bit. "Well, I met up with someone down here who would also like this whole thing closed. We have a list of different places that we need to explore. Once we return, we would be happy to come back to see you and discuss our options." Dennis explained.

"That sounds wonderful. We look forward to seeing you again. Anything we can provide you with, you're welcome to." Glenn said. Dennis thanked him and told him that they would be in touch soon.

For the rest of the afternoon and into the night, Dennis and Brett discussed how they were going to go about their adventure. They decided to start off with a visit to Arkansas in the morning, since that was the closest one to where they were. In the morning they made sure they had everything they would need for their long drive.

At the same time Amy was on her way to the airport to catch her ten AM flight back to New England. She got out of bed at around seven thirty, before anyone else in the house was up. She took a walk to the local coffee shop to call a cab. The cab brought her to the airport. During the whole ride Amy had an uncomfortable nervous feeling in her stomach.

She was let out in front of the terminal and she had to find her way from there. With a horrible lonely feeling and her eyes filled with tears, she walked through the airport in a daze looking for gate twelve.

It seemed like an eternity for her as she tried to pull herself together and count the gates, as she approached gate number seven. She tried to count in her confused mind the amount of gates that were left until she reached number twelve. That seemed to be a chore of it's own in her emotional state.

As she walked, she counted the gates in her mind. She reached number ten and then eleven. Part of her wanted to turn back and head to her cousin Linda's house but the other part was determined to break free of her mother's rules and what she felt were laws.

Amy stopped and looked up at the sign that said "Gate 12", next to it was a clock that said "9:36". Some of the passengers were already boarding. "This is it. I am off to start my new life of freedom." She thought to herself, as she headed toward the back of the line of boarding passengers.

She looked toward the front of the line and she couldn't believe her eyes. She felt a sudden relief and comfort that cleared away any feelings she thought of as freedom.

Standing by the front of the line was her mother, Rosa. Amy left the line and walked towards Rosa. Now she realized where she should be and wanted to be.

They gave each other a big hug and held each other close for a few minutes. Afterwards, Rosa took Amy out for breakfast where she explained how she was only trying to protect her and how what may seem as being strict was only making sure Amy's best interest was being considered.

Rosa joked that it is not easy to put one over on her. She checked her bank account a couple of days before and noticed the plane ticket charge. That is how she was able to get the details of the flight.

Amy explained that she wasn't stealing and the airfare was under her alarm clock. "I may have raised a sneak but at least you're not a thief." Rosa joked.

Amy almost asked about her father during this time of closeness but she thought about it for a minute and figured that would only ruin it. She had been thinking about him a little more than usual the last few weeks, since she came across an old picture that Rosa doesn't like to talk about.

Chapter Fourteen
"Arkansas to Oklahoma"

September 2003

Dennis and Brett arrived at the church in Arkansas and just as they expected, it seemed identical to the others. They both went inside to have a look around.

"I don't want to stay in here too long. This is not my kind of place." Brett said as he glanced around at the dreariness of the church. "Don't worry, I don't like it anymore than you do." Dennis whispered, as they took a seat toward the back.

Dennis closed a mass book and as he attempted to place it in his jacket he felt a presence behind him. "May I help you with something gentlemen?" A voice asked from behind them. Dennis turned around and thought for a moment that he was back in South Carolina. It was another young priest who came across like Father Servat.

"No sir, father. We just stopped in on our drive through town." Dennis said. "Oh, visitors, we always welcome visitors. Where are you gentlemen from?" The priest asked. "Kentucky." Brett answered nervously.

"Yes, we're from Kentucky and we are headed down to Texas for a funeral. A dear friend of ours has passed and we stop every so often to pray. I hope it's not a bother father." Dennis quickly made up the story.

"Oh, I am sorry to hear that my son. Please take all of the time you need. If I can do anything for you, I will be back in my office. Just come and get me. My name is Father Nuntius." He said, as he walked off.

"Pretty quick thinking. I almost started to laugh when you said, bother father." Brett whispered. "Oh, you caught that too? I realized how funny it sounded when it was too late." Dennis said, as he put the mass book in his pocket and they headed out.

They got into the car and drove away from that place as quickly as possible. "That was a close one. Didn't you feel bad about lying to a priest?" Brett asked. "I would have, if I felt like he was a sincere priest. There was something about him that I didn't like. He may be a big part of what has been going on lately." Dennis suggested.

"Oh no, what did I do wrong?" Brett asked, as he looked in his rearview mirror. There were police lights flashing behind them on the quiet interstate. Brett pulled the car over to the side of the road and Dennis told him to stay cool.

"Sorry officer. Was I speeding?" Brett asked, when the officer approached the car door. "Can I see your license and registration sir?" The policeman asked, as Brett fumbled through his wallet. "Here, here you are sir." Brett said, as he trembled. "Excuse me while I run this sir. I will be right back." The officer said, as he walked back to his car.

"What did I do? What is going to happen?" Brett asked Dennis. "Just relax, he's probably giving you a hard time because of your Kentucky plates. You didn't do anything wrong." Dennis explained, as the officer headed back toward them.

"Mr. Delancy, this says you're from Kentucky. What brings you down to Arkansas?" The officer asked. "We're just on a road trip to visit a friend in Texas." Brett said. "I see, so, you're a church going man Mr. Delancy, are ya?" The officer asked. "Yes, sir, why do you ask?" Brett asked.

"Only because you left the church in such a hurry. Is everything all right at the church?" He asked. "Oh, yes sir. We just stopped to say a prayer for a friend." Brett said, as Dennis hit himself in the forehead with his hand.

"Okay Mr. Delancy, you gentlemen have a safe trip through our fine state." The policeman said, as he handed Brett his license back and walked to his car.

Brett waited for the officer to pull away first but he could see that wasn't going to happen. "You better go first Mr. Delancy, he's not moving." Dennis said sarcastically. "I was hoping he would go first but I guess I have to." Brett said, as he pulled away.

"I thought your last name was Black?" Dennis inquired. "How many people do you know that use their real last name on an e-mail?" Brett asked.

"Yea, I guess you're right. So, do you feel like cruising straight on into Oklahoma?" Dennis asked. "That will be fine, as long as you drive the rest of the way. That cop made me a nervous wreck." Brett suggested.

"Sounds good to me. Let's switch after we eat something." Dennis replied. They pulled into the next service area for a quick dinner and some rest.

Back in South Carolina, since Rosa and Amy were getting along better than ever, Amy told Rosa that if she really feels that close to Dennis, she wouldn't mind if she gave him a call to patch things up. Rosa explained the little fight she had with Dennis to Amy. Amy didn't want to come between their friendship.

"I am glad that you suggested that sweet heart. I have been thinking about calling him. I was a little out of line. Maybe I'll give him a call in the morning." Rosa said.

"Good. I really don't hate him. I think I was just looking for a place to direct my anger, when it should have been directed at that jerk I was falling in love with. When you talk to Dennis, tell him I said hello." Amy requested.

"Speaking of that jerk, wasn't someone supposed to meet you at the airport when you landed?" Rosa asked. "Oh let him wait." Amy replied with anger towards her old friends.

In Boston, Rayzer was at Logan airport most of the day waiting for Amy. He watched her flight land and a few others after it. After four and a half-hours of sitting around the airport, he was steamed. Not only was he mad about the waiting but he also wanted for murder and he was taking a big risk hanging out in a public place. He tried calling Amy all night but she didn't answer the phone.

He was able to get in touch with David, who was still on probation from the dreaded McDonalds heist. That was what it came to be known as to the group.

David told Razer that the guys were able to tear up Dennis' office and if he wants Dennis to disappear that could happen next. "Just say the word and that private dick is history." David said. "Let's just be cool. I still gotta be hiding and your ass is being watched all the time. When I'm ready, I'll let you know." Rayzer said.

"That's why I have the boys taking care of the shit. I ain't getting my hands dirtier, but I'll wait for your word. When are we gonna see you again?" David asked. "When things cool down, I'll be in touch. Just keep your eye on that guy until then, and if you see or hear anything about that bitch Amy, get the word to me however you can. Her ass wasn't on that plane." Rayzer angrily stated.

"That's messed up. I'll let you know when I hear something. Be cool." David said. "All right, peace." Razer replied, as he went back into hiding by the water tower.

Dennis and Brett made it to Oklahoma in the middle of the night. They stayed at a motel to get a little sleep before their visit to the next church.

Dennis woke up a few minutes after twelve noon. He decided to check his voice mails one more time. There was a message that he had been hoping to hear. "Hi Dennis, it's me, Rosa. First off, I would just like to say sorry for snapping at you the other day. I hope you don't hate me. I'd like to get together whenever possible. Give me a call." She went on joking about how he probably threw her number away, so she gave it to him again.

Dennis was extremely happy to hear that message and he planned to give her a call back as soon as he finished his mission in Oklahoma.

The next message was a frantic one, from Dr. Hynes. "Dennis, it's me Arty, something is wrong. I tried getting in touch with Bert a few times over the last couple of days and I haven't been able to. Anyway, remember the teacher that he met when him and I took that trip to England? Her name is Lynn. She has also been trying to get in touch with him. She is staying with a friend in New York and she was planning on visiting him this week. Well I don't want to take up too much space on this voice mail thing, so just call me when you get a chance." Dr. Hynes went on.

Dennis was surprised by both messages. He thought that maybe the reason he hasn't heard from Bert was because of something bigger than their argument. Now he was getting a little worried about him.

Brett was just waking up as he let out a loud yawn from the next room. "Good you're up. Let's get a move on, so I can make some important calls when we get back." Dennis said. Brett gave him a confused look as he stretched his arms out and yawned again.

Dennis explained the important phone calls that he had to make to Rosa, Dr. Hynes and Bert, as they drove to the next church.

Brett suggested he make the phone calls during the drive. Dennis told him that depending on what they had to say, it would probably only distract him from the case at hand.

Chapter Fifteen
"One phone call"

Dennis and Brett arrived at the church in Oklahoma and went through their regular routine. Again the church resembled the others and they took a look around. They spoke with a woman who was a member of the church. Like the other worshipers, she appeared to be focused only on the church.

She noticed that they were new comers and she tried to get them to join the parish. She spoke of Father Ducto and what an inspirational change he brought to the church.

Dennis listened to see if she had any valuable information for his case. The woman did convince him that the various priests he had been meeting all seemed to have a common interest.

The woman was called away by her friend. "I hope to see you here real soon." She said, as she walked away slowly. Dennis and Brett were taken back by the woman's eerie presence. They went back about their business and Dennis swiped another mass book and put it in his jacket pocket.

"So, who are you gonna call first?" Brett asked when they got back into the car. "I think it's going to be Rosa. You should come down to South Carolina with me to meet her. While we're down there, we can meet up with Glenn and Tara and follow up on that church to see why it keeps changing back and forth." Dennis suggested.

"That sounds like a plan. I would like to stop by the store first and check on, uh oh, not again." Brett said, as he looked in the rear view mirror.

"Oh shit! That can't be for us. There's too many of them." Dennis said, as he turned around to see close to twenty police cars behind them with their lights flashing. "Should I pull over? This is crazy! I have never seen so many police cars in one place before!" Brett exclaimed, as he became very nervous.

"Just slow down and stay to the right. Let them pass, they have to be after someone else." Dennis said, as Brett proceeded to do so. "It's not working. They're not passing. They're staying behind us. They're slowing down. What did we do wrong?" Brett went on in a panic.

"Pull over! Pull over and show your hands!" A voice said from the police speaker. "Just do what they say. They probably have us confused with someone else." Dennis said, as Brett pulled to the side and stopped the car.

The police cars surrounded them and the officers started making their way to the car with their guns drawn. "Get out of the car! Get out of the car!" One of them yelled as, Dennis and Brett walked out onto the pavement with their hands in the air.

"Get on the ground! Now!" The officer yelled, as both of them laid down with their hands behind their necks. They were both cuffed and thrown into the back of two separate police cars. An officer with a pad and pen sat in the front seat of the car that Dennis was in.

"Would it be a bad idea to ask what this is all about?" Dennis asked. "Not at all but you probably know more than I do. This whole arrest comes from a higher power. I don't really know what you did but the government wants you pretty bad." The officer said just before he read Dennis his rights.

A short distance away, in another police car, Brett was begging the officer to explain what was going on. "All I can tell you is, someone doesn't think you should be visiting the churches you have been to lately." The officer said, as he put his seat belt on and headed to the station.

Back in New England, Dr. Hynes was sitting in his living room watching television with his wife as the phone rang. It was Lynn from the school in England. She explained that she was still worried about Bert and she attempted to find his laboratory but she wasn't having much luck.

"Where are you now?" Dr. Hynes asked. She explained where she was as best she could. "If you were any closer, you would be in his living room." He joked. She insisted that she looked all over in the area and she did not see the building that Bert described to her.

"This doesn't sound right. Are you going to be there a while?" He asked. "I don't know what to do, I borrowed my friend's car so that I could maybe surprise Bert. Now it seems like a waste." Lynn explained.

"You got me curious. I have been worried about him too. Now I am also worried about Dennis, another friend of ours. I called him to ask about Bert and he hasn't returned my calls either. I am about an hour away from Bert's place. Can I meet you there?" Dr. Hynes asked.

"Sure, I guess so. I will just call my friend and explain what I am doing." Lynn said. "Okay, I'll see you in about an hour." Dr. Hynes said. He explained to his wife what was going on and asked if she wanted to go for the ride. She declined and told him to be careful. She was content sitting in her rocking chair crocheting.

A little more than an hour later, Lynn was sitting in the car looking around in fear. She jumped at every small sound. A strange movement came from a bush outside. Figuring she was just as safe outside of the car, she decided to have a look.

As she walked closer to the bush, she trembled. She pulled some of the leaves back to one side and took a look inside the bush. The whole bush shook as she put her hand over her heart and jumped back a few feet.

After some rustling, a rabbit ran from the bush. Lynn caught her breath and smiled with relief. She was startled once again when a car pulled in next to hers. She was relieved to see that it was Dr. Hynes. It felt as if she was waiting hours for him to show up.

Much to Dr. Hynes' surprise, Bert's laboratory was gone. The lot where it used to stand looked as if the building never existed. Dr. Hynes walked back and forth over the baron ground where the laboratory once stood.

"This is unreal. I feel like I am in a dream. How the hell does a building just disappear?" Dr. Hynes questioned loudly to Lynn, who was leaning against her friend's car nodding her head.

"I am shocked but I can't completely share in your disbelief. I have never seen the laboratory before. Maybe we are in the wrong place." She suggested.

"No, this is absolutely the right place. I have been here a number of times. I know all of the land marks that surrounded the area and they are still here." Dr. Hynes explained.

The two of them stood there unable to understand the situation as Dr. Hynes attempted to call both Bert and Dennis repeatedly, only to get their voice mails again and again.

"This has to have something to do with them visiting those satanic churches. I knew they were going too far with that stuff." Dr. Hynes said. "What are you talking about? Who is into Satanism? Did I miss something?" Lynn asked.

Dr. Hynes explained all about the churches that he was aware of. He told Lynn that he is afraid of the whole situation and he feels that Bert and Dennis should have stayed away from that evilness. He informed Lynn that now he is also worried that something may happen to him, since he was with them at the church in Rhode Island.

"This is a little more than I can handle. I am just going to head back to New York, where my biggest worry is having my purse snatched. Here is my phone number, only call me if you have good news. I don't think I can handle anything else besides good news regarding this." Lynn said nervously.

"I can't say I blame you. I am probably going to lay low for a while myself. I hope I can call you with some good news. Take care of yourself." Dr. Hynes said to Lynn, as she rushed to the car and hurried to the interstate. She drove frantically while continuously looking over her shoulders.

Lynn never experienced anything as strange as she did that day. Most of her life she was protected and sheltered. The scariest excitement she ever witnessed before this was the fire at her school.

Dr. Hynes made it back home and explained the disappearance of Bert's lab to his wife. She was shocked at the story.

Dr. Hynes contemplated going to Dennis' office. He wondered if anything strange was going on over there also. He decided against visiting there at the moment. He would rather let things make sense on their own before getting himself involved. He spent most of the night awake, thinking about what was going on.

The next morning in South Carolina, Rosa explained to Linda how she finally broke down and called Dennis. "Do you think it was a mistake? He should have called me back by now. He must be angrier than I thought." She said.

"Maybe he's just really busy. You know how involved his job is." Linda responded. "I hope you're right. I'll give him one more day, if I don't hear from him by then, I'll forget all about him." Rosa said.

"Yea, like you could do that. Just wait for him to call you back. That's what you really want to do." Linda answered back. "I hate to admit it, but you're right. There is something about him that makes me think of him all the time. I just hope he is okay, and I hope he calls me back." Rosa explained.

"Well, for what it's worth, he seems like a reasonable guy. He's the kind of guy that will stay in touch. Besides, it appears that he is interested in you also." Linda said comforting. "Thanks Linda. You're a big help." Rosa replied; as Amy came down to have breakfast with them.

Back in Oklahoma, Dennis and Brett were being served hard bagels and cold coffee in their separate cells.

"Can I ask a stupid question?" Dennis asked the officer who was serving the coffee. "You just did. Don't tell me you want a second bagel." The officer responded. "My teeth couldn't handle the first one. I just wanted to find out about my one phone call. Will I be getting one?" He asked.

"I'm sorry, you and your friend are in here for something special and I am really curious to find out what it is. You are guests of the United States Government and they don't want you in contact with anyone on the outside. In an hour or so, you're going to be transported to a government building for questioning or whatever it is that they do. All I can do is offer you a second bagel or more coffee. No phone calls." The officer explained.

Dennis thought about explaining how he was a private investigator but he figured that wouldn't make a difference at this point. He just sat in his cell quietly, trying to figure out why he was wanted by the government.

Brett sat still in the corner of his cell, just staring at the wall in disbelief. He wondered to himself if Dennis had done something prior to them meeting, which could have caused them to be locked up.

After a couple of hours, guards escorted two secret service agents to the cells. Dennis and Brett were taken out and brought to separate limousines.

After a half-hour ride, once again they were escorted to separate rooms. Again it was a waiting game. They each sat hand cuffed and nervous.

Brett was visited first by two secret service agents. They questioned him for over an hour about how he met up with Dennis and what their interest was in the churches. Brett told them everything they needed to know. He explained how Dennis sent him the e-mail asking about the churches in the articles and that Dennis wanted him to begin traveling around the country with him visiting those churches.

The agents wanted to know if the e-mail he was talking about was saved on Brett's computer. Brett assured them that all of their conversations on the Internet were still on his hard drive.

"If you want to come home with me, I will show you everything on the computer." He said. "That won't be necessary. Give us your address and that computer will be here within the next couple of hours." One of the agents said.

Brett gave his address and then he was sent into another room for a psychological and a physical examination. They put him to sleep for the physical portion. They checked his body for scars or anything out of the normal.

By the time he woke, his computer had arrived and the agents were examining the e-mails. They were also going through everything that was found in his car, such as, Dennis' scrapbook and mass books.

Since everything checked out all right with Brett, he was taken home and warned that he would be under government surveillance. He didn't mind, he was just happy to be released. He swore to himself that he would have nothing to do with Dennis ever again.

While Brett was on his way home, it was Dennis' turn to be interrogated. He was slightly nervous, but much more laid back than Brett was. He figured he was clean and there had to be some kind of a mistake.

His story connected with Brett's and he explained how he was involved in a case that involved the churches. They talked for quite a while and Dennis' computer was on its way there also. Then it was time for his psychological and physical examinations.

Something turned up on his physical portion that caused the agents some concern. They met outside to discuss it while Dennis slept.

"This is the guy. I didn't buy that BS private investigator crap from the beginning." The first agent stated. "I can't believe anyone would go to these lengths for any cause. We are going to be on the A list after nailing this sick son of a bitch." The other agent replied with a proud smirk.

G. Novitsky

Chapter Sixteen
"Enter Charlie"

While Dennis was sleeping, they moved him into a maximum-security sanitarium across town. They also put him in a straight jacket.

When he woke up he couldn't move his arms. In a confused state, he tried to stand up and move around, only to fall on his face. "Help! Help! What the hell are you doing to me? Why am I here?" He yelled, as he looked around his padded room.

He was extremely confused and he started to think that this might have had something to do with the death of Amy's boyfriend, Rick. He also felt as if he was living some sort of double life. Maybe this was his second personality that he was meeting for the first time. Strange things can happen to a person who is being cut off from the outside world, even on their first day.

"Psssssst. Calm down." A whisper came from a small barred window on one of the walls. Dennis was finally able to get up on his feet. He walked slowly over to the window, as he shook nervously.

On the other side was a short man with long hair and a long mustache and beard. He was wearing a long white robe. "Where are we?" Dennis asked the man very quietly.

"We are in hell on earth Mr. Carved." The man replied. "What do you mean? Who are you?" Dennis asked. "I am Charlie. We will be roommates soon. They always send the new people to me. Been hoping

for a lady but they'll never mex the sixes around here."
Charlie babbled.

"Mex the sixes?" Dennis asked. "They don't let the
mens and the ladies share rooms. It's a rule. You have
to obey the rules." Charlie tried to explain. "Oh, oh I
see, you mean, mix the sexes." Dennis replied.

"That's what I said. It don't matter no way, cause I
am going to be free soon. I tried two times but they
caught me in my tree. They say, charms a third, right?"
Charlie went on.

"Yes Charlie, right, three times a charm." Dennis
replied. "I would take you with me to the bright place
but if we both go, we only get caught, Carved. Uh oh,
Mel is here. I can't talk to you now. Come to window
eatins done." Charlie said, as he turned around to be
greeted by the orderly. Dennis turned around and wept
with his head in his folded arms.

The next day in New England, Dr. Hynes was
losing it. All he could think about was Bert and
Dennis. He wasn't able to make sense of Bert's lab
disappearing and he felt like he just had to check on
Dennis' office.

Once again he explained to his wife that something
was going on and he couldn't just sit around and let it
happen. He didn't invite his wife for the ride this time.
He just left.

The ride took close to forty-five minutes. It was a
bit closer than Bert's lab but in the opposite direction.

He parked in front of the building and went up to
the third floor to the office. The door was locked and
the shade on the window was shut. He wasn't able to
see inside. He knocked on the door repeatedly and
there was no answer.

His overpowering concern got the best of him and he broke the window to get inside. The office was completely bare except for a couple of empty boxes on the floor. He was sure that there was something abnormal going on after seeing the condition of the office.

He looked out of the window, down at the street and held on to the windowsill. He stared down for a moment when all of a sudden he felt a canvas sack being placed over his head. He quickly attempted to fight it off as he was pummeled by punches.

"You shouldn't have brought your stupid ass back here, bitch!" A voice said. "Please stop!" Dr. Hynes groaned, as he fell to the floor. "You gotta pay for the shit you did!" Another voice yelled, as a hand went through his pockets.

Dr. Hynes was continuously battered until the intruders suddenly made a quick getaway, as if they felt they would be caught if they stayed too long. Dr. Hynes was left unconscious, as a smoke bomb went off in the office.

Back in South Carolina, Rosa was focused on the television news. Some of the churches were being shown. The news broadcaster mentioned how there was a church in Idaho that was practicing extremely abnormal activities. Complaints had also been pouring in to the local police department about the church and a priest named Father Ponde.

"Linda, come here! Look at this!" She yelled. "What? What is going on?" Linda asked, as she ran in spilling her soda.

"It's Dennis' investigation! They are talking about the churches! They mentioned Idaho. I don't recall

Dennis mentioning Idaho though." Rosa said, as she remained glued to the television.

The broadcaster also spoke about Oklahoma and how there were strange occurrences there as well. He spoke briefly about an arrest in that area but it was not confirmed that the arrest was related to the activities at the churches.

The story was mainly about the worshipers in the churches being riled up and having plans to sacrifice their leader. For some reason or another, the leader needed to be executed by the churchgoers. The report was very brief. It wasn't easy for them to get details regarding the situation.

"See, I told you Dennis was probably too involved in his work to call you." Linda said. "It sure looks that way. This church thing seems to be getting a little out of hand. I wonder if Dennis has been working on the ones in Oklahoma and Idaho. I hope he is safe." Rosa commented.

Back at the sanitarium, Dennis had an orderly checking on him. Dennis attempted to get information from him but the orderly was uncooperative. "What are you doing to me? This is against the law! I have a life to get back to! I am innocent!" Dennis yelled as the orderly walked out of the room.

"You can have this room to yourself when I leave. I am going to make myself gone soon. You can stay here then." Charlie said from the window.

"Charlie? Charlie is that you?" Dennis whispered, as he made his way over toward the window. "Yes Carved, it's me. I will be gone soon." Charlie said.

"Where are you going Charlie?" Dennis asked. "I had ten years here. I don't like the ten years. I tried to make myself die two times. Charms a third. I am going to do it right this time. This place is not good to me. I have to leave. You'll be in my room soon." Charlie said.

"How are you going to do it?" Dennis asked. "Sorry Carved, I can't tell you. That's secret. It will be better." Charlie said.

"You're probably right. This place does seem worse than death. I hope you get your wish one-day, as morbid as that sounds. Hey Charlie, why do you keep calling me Carved?" Dennis asked, as the orderly came back into Dennis' room with two agents.

"Hello Dennis, how do you feel?" One of them asked. "Confused, I don't understand why I am here." He answered. "We would like to talk to you for a moment." The other one said, as the orderly took the straight jacket off of Dennis.

They walked him down the hallway into a small room with a desk and a couple of chairs. The room was cold and dimly lit. One of the agents stood by the door. The other one sat behind the desk and offered Dennis the other chair.

"Did you think you were going to take over the country Dennis?" The agent asked, as he opened a notebook. "I don't know what you mean sir." Dennis responded.

"Our records tell us, you have been brainwashing thousands of naive church goers to follow your word. What are your plans after they are trained?" He asked.

"I wasn't brainwashing anyone. I was just investigating. Why don't you people believe me?" Dennis asked, as he tried to explain once again that he was working on a case involving the churches.

The agents spoke to him for a while, trying to get information about his plans and the new religion. Dennis stuck to his story and insisted that he didn't have any information for them. They informed Dennis, because of his lack of cooperation, he would be living on the grounds for a long time.

After their meeting, the agents decided that Dennis was not violent or dangerous, and just as Charlie said, Dennis became his new roommate.

When Dennis walked into his new room, Charlie was fast asleep in his bed. Dennis lied down on the other bed with tears in his eyes. He stared at the ceiling with a distraught look about him.

Chapter Seventeen
"Buzzing about Carved and the Beam Phone"

Up in New England, Dr. Hynes was discovered by local police, knocked out in Dennis' office. The police had an ambulance on the scene right away.

He woke up in the hospital with his wife and two police officers standing over him. "Where the hell am I?" He asked, as he started to come to. "You're in the hospital darling. These police officers found you beaten with a bag over your head at your friend's office. What happened and why do you smell like smoke?" Mrs. Hynes asked.

The criminals stole everything he had on him except his ID card. "I don't know. All I can remember is a very strange dream I had. Bert's house was in it. Actually, it wasn't in it. It was the land his house was built on. The house disappeared." He said.

"Who is Bert?" One of the officers asked. "He is a friend of Arthur's who hasn't been around in a while. Maybe the same creeps got to him. Arthur went to his house the other day and it was gone. That's why he went to check on this other friend's office." Mrs. Hynes explained.

"Elsie, how did you know about my dream?" Dr. Hynes asked, in his weakened state. "That wasn't a dream, that really happened. You met that woman friend of Bert's there and his laboratory was missing, remember?" Mrs. Hynes explained, as Dr. Hynes started to doze off again.

The police officers were very interested in the story about Bert's house. Mrs. Hynes told them all that she knew. She also informed them of the church stories that she was aware of.

"That sounds like the case down south that they are trying to keep quiet. I have an ex-partner who is on the job in that area. I'd like to see what he can find out about it. Here, please take my card and have your husband call me when he is up to talking." The officer said, as he handed the card to Mrs. Hynes. She thanked them as they left the room.

Back at the sanitarium, Charlie woke from his nap and noticed Dennis lying in the bed next to him. "Carved? I knew you was going to stay with me. My snoring kept you awake, right? I wish I didn't snore. Some people snore." Charlie rambled. "No, no you didn't snore. You're a quiet sleeper. Now you can tell me why you call me Carved." Dennis demanded.

"I know, I'm sorry about the snoring. You're not the first time complaining to me. Some people snore. They said you are Carved. They said; the new guy is Carved. You're the new guy, you're Carved. Charlie said.

"I would love to know where that came from. Did they say anything else?" Dennis asked. "I can't tell the secrets. They said you are gonna stay here forever." Charlie told him.

"Charlie, you can call me Dennis. That would be fine. Okay?" Dennis suggested. "Okay, but my teeth don't hurt. Do yours hurt? They hurt sometimes, now they're fine." Charlie went on.

"Charlie, is there anyway I can make a phone call from this place?" Dennis asked. "Yes, phone calls are easy, except for, I don't have someone to call. Do you want the beam phone? I can get you the beam phone if you want it, Dentist." Charlie said.

"I'm probably going to kick myself for asking but, what is the beam phone Charlie? Can I call home with it?" Dennis asked.

"All of the guys call home on the beam phone. You can call home on the beam phone, Dentist. I'll get it for you when I see Denver. He holds the beam phone and he says never to tell the orglies, cause they would take it away. Do you make promise not to tell? Then I can get it for you, Dentist." Charlie rambled.

"You can bet your special ass I won't tell. When are you going to see Denver? I would love to use this beam phone. Please God, make it a real phone." Dennis requested.

Charlie told him that he usually sees Denver before bedtime. The patients called it a beam phone because it was a small cellular phone. They were not really up on technology. One of the guys just named it that, probably because he thought it was sending out a laser beam to the person on the other end.

It was a perfectly functioning cellular phone. Denver's brother gave it to him. He made sure that Denver kept it a secret from the orderlies. Denver's brother would change the battery once a week when he came to visit.

Denver's brother didn't care for Denver being in that home but it was the least expensive way for him to get the care he needed.

During dinner, Dennis met Denver. He was no worse off than Charlie, except for his history of violence on top of his brain damage. Denver was an inch or two taller than Charlie, and quite a bit wider.

He weighed close to two hundred and twenty pounds and he wasn't the cleanest of people.

Dennis went back to the room before Charlie because the orderlies were watching him so closely because it was his first night out of his straight jacket. After television time, Charlie returned to the room with the beam phone. "Gotta get it back at breakfast time. Denver gets ascared." Charlie said, as he handed the phone to Dennis.

"Sure thing. Let's just hope this thing works. Thanks Charlie." Dennis said. "Welcome Dentist. Breakfast I give it back, then he will trust you too. You can have it more times then." Charlie said.

Dennis agreed and he took the phone into the bathroom. He told Charlie to knock if anyone came. "Come on, beam phone!" Dennis said, as he dialed Rosa's phone number. He almost didn't remember her number, it has been so long since he called her.

"Hello?" Rosa's voice answered. "Rosa, it's me, Dentist, I mean Dennis. I'll explain that later. I can't really talk. I just wanted to let you know that I got your message and I am in a lot of trouble." Dennis whispered.

"Oh my God! What is happening?" She asked. She was thrilled to hear his voice and at the same time she was filled with concern.

"I am in a sanitarium. Don't ask. They think I have something to do with organizing those churches. Can you do me a favor and call Dr. Hynes?" Dennis asked, as he gave her Dr. Hynes' phone number.

He explained as much as he could and let her know he would call her when he had a more convenient opportunity. He told her about the beam phone and how he wanted to keep his privileges to it.

Rosa explained that the churches were on the news and that there was talk about sacrificing the leader. Now that Dennis was thought to be the leader, their concerns grew. They quickly ended their conversation and hoped to speak again soon.

Dennis walked out of the bathroom and noticed Charlie sitting on the bed extremely nervous. "Is everything all right Charlie?" He asked. "No, it's three fives till nine o'clock." Charlie said. Dennis looked at the clock and figured out that meant fifteen minutes to nine.

"Here, take the beam phone back and be extra careful with it, I'm going to need it again soon. What's wrong with nine o'clock?" Dennis asked. "Nine o'clock is buzzing time. You better hold the beam phone till after buzzing time. I don't want them to find it at buzzing time." Charlie explained.

"What is buzzing time Charlie?" Dennis asked. "Buzzing time is a secret. You keep the beam phone till I come back from buzzing time." Charlie requested. "There sure is a shit load of secrets going on in this place." Dennis mumbled to himself, as he put the phone under the dresser.

Rosa tried calling Dr. Hynes a few times that night. She was only able to get his voice mail. When the morning arrived, Mrs. Hynes returned the calls. Rosa introduced herself over the phone and explained the situation that Dennis was in. Mrs. Hynes was stunned, and she explained what happened to her husband.

Dr. Hynes was doing much better and he met with the officer who was looking into the church situation.

It was time for the followers to find their leader and sacrifice him for the better of the world. The word was out around the new found religious community that their leader was Dennis and they had his room number at the sanitarium. They were working on a way to get to him.

Later that night, Dennis was able to get the beam phone once again. Most of the orderlies were busy in some kind of a meeting, so Dennis had a little extra time for phone calls. He decided to give Dr. Hynes a call. They finally had a chance to talk after all of the confusion.

Dennis informed Dr. Hynes of his situation in more detail than he was already told and Dr. Hynes told Dennis what happened back at his office.

"I wanted to tell you that I moved out of that office but I never had the chance with all of the insanity going on." Dennis explained. "Insanity? Remarkable choice of words, speaking of insanity, I was given a phone number and now would be a mighty fine moment to have a conference call. Would you mind if I gave it a shot?" Dr. Hynes asked.

"I don't know if this is the right time to play, 'This is your life.' Can you give me a hint?" Dennis responded.

"Supposedly, Bert has been trying to contact us. I received a letter in the mail and it had a phone number." Dr. Hynes explained. "What are you waiting for? Get him on the phone!" Dennis demanded.

There was a pause in the phone conversation, as Dennis felt a strong nervous feeling in his stomach. He thought he would never hear from his old friend Bert again.

"Hello old fool. Got yourself in some trouble once again, did you?" Bert questioned, as Dr. Hynes conferenced him in. "Unbelievable! I thought I would never hear your voice again and now I am talking to you from a mental institution, on a friggen beam phone. You can't plan these things." Dennis went on.

"Maybe you can." Bert said, and then there was a long pause. "What do you mean by that?" Dr. Hynes asked. "Well, it wasn't exactly planned this way, but there was a plan. You weren't supposed to be the leader, however you made me promote you due to your interference." Bert explained.

"This isn't funny. What the hell are you talking about?" Dennis asked nervously. "Now, now Dennis old boy. You should sit down and control yourself. My guess is there is still a straight jacket near by with your name on it." Bert commented, accompanied by a small sinister laugh. "Okay, I'm calm. Tell me what is going on Bert!" Dennis demanded.

"You spoiled my plan Dennis. You involved yourself too much. It reached the point where I had to save myself and let someone else take the fall. You see, the whole Domi On The Skull, was a late addition to the plan. I had to think fast. They were going to close in on me. Now I can take some of what I created and expand it in an underground sort of way." Bert explained.

"You are absolutely despicable! What in God's name is Domi On The Skull?" Dennis asked.

"They didn't tell you? I thought for sure, that would have been the first thing to come up in your interrogation. You're carved Dennis. Carved, deep in your skull are the letters D.O.M.I. I am supposed to be

Domi, quite frankly, I still am. You will be gone in a couple of days." Bert said, as Dennis felt the back of his head where Bert stitched him. That is when Bert decided to put the word out to sacrifice the leader, Dennis.

"You son of a bitch! You destroyed my life! I thought you cared about me when you stitched my head!" Dennis said, as his eyes filled up with tears.

"I did care about you Dennis, until you got too close. You were going to solve the case sooner or later. I had to change the course a bit. I apologize if you are not happy with my work." Bert said sarcastically.

"What about all of the nice things you did? Going to the school in England, teaching the kids, saving them from the fire? What about the guy on the airplane, The guy with the panic attack?" Dr. Hynes questioned.

"The school? The fire was my doing. The classroom next door taught a silly religion. That room burned like gunpowder, now those kids will think twice about believing in what went on in there. As for George on the airplane, who do you think was kind enough to hit old Dennis over the head with the bottle? That was good old panic attack George.

You see, a good sheep should have a weakness. George's weakness is that he let his panic attacks control him. That made him the perfect follower. He would do anything I requested of him, and he still does." Bert explained. He exchanged phone numbers with George on the plane without Dr. Hynes noticing.

"You are truly a sick twisted son of a bitch! Does this sort of sickness give you a boost? How do you feel after seeing that you took it as far as you did?" Dr. Hynes asked.

"It's kinda like the first time, as a young boy, pleasuring yourself. Do you remember your first time Arty? You feel guilty at first. You know what you're doing is wrong. Once you get started you don't know how it will end, but you have to keep going. When you are all finished, you look down at the mess you created and some disturbed part of your brain makes you proud to call it your own." Bert proudly stated.

"You are a sick bastard! That disturbed part represents your entire brain. Dennis, I can't listen to anymore of his shit!" Dr. Hynes said.

"Let me leave you with one final thought. First, don't try to reach me on this line again. It will be destroyed. I just wanted one last chat with you fellows. There are two things my mother instilled in my head before she passed on. One was, if I didn't want to burn in hell when I die, I should make everyone love me. The second was, if I can't fall asleep, I should always count my sheep. I think my new found religion has brought me both." Bert said, as he hung up the phone.

There was a long pause. "Dennis, are you still there?" Dr. Hynes asked. "That is why Charlie called me Carved. That insane monster carved letters into my skull. That's why I am here No one is going to believe that I had that carved into my skull without my consent." Dennis went on.

"What are you going to do?" Dr. Hynes asked. "What can I do? He won the game. I am going to let his followers take me and finish the game. I love you Arty. Tell Rosa I loved her from the moment I met her but I couldn't work up the nerve to tell her." Dennis requested, as he hung up the phone.

Dr. Hynes tried to stop Dennis from hanging up but he was unsuccessful. He lied awake all night crying and trying to think of a way to help Dennis out of the mess he was in.

Dennis returned the phone to Charlie when he came back from his nine o'clock Buzzing. The two of them spent most of the night talking. Dennis was able to get Charlie to explain what the nine o'clock Buzzing was.

It turned out that three of the orderlies found enjoyment in treating some of the weaker patients with unscheduled shock therapy. They would pick one of them at nine o'clock each night to hook up to the machine and shock them for ten minutes at a time.

Usually after they tortured the patient, they would retire to the orderly recreation center for a soak in the hot tub. It was kind of a ritual for them. None of the patients were supposed to be in the recreation center, but the orderlies allowed Denver in to fetch them towels and change the radio stations on the portable stereo every now and again. That was just another way for them to abuse a patient, Denver didn't know any better.

When Dennis learned of the Buzzing's, he was enraged. The orderlies didn't like Dennis as it was because he was able to think for himself. Now they were aware that Dennis had some knowledge of the Buzzing's and that brought more hatred toward him.

It turned out that the same orderlies were scheduled the next night to keep an eye on Dennis. An order came from the agents on the case because they were expecting the worshipers to pay Dennis a visit soon.

The orderlies figured this was their chance to get Dennis out of there before he caused any trouble. They decided to turn the other way as soon as anything goes down with the worshipers.

G. Novitsky

Chapter Eighteen
"To Die for Freedom"

October 2003

The next evening, as the sun started to set, Dennis had a feeling that this was going to be the night for the visit. He left a note for Denver and then he spent all of the time he could with Charlie. The two of them sat in the front yard on a bench, under a tree a couple hundred feet from the road.

They spoke about happier times in each of their lives. Dennis spoke about his old friends from the neighborhood and how they always watched each other's backs. He mentioned that not even they would be able to get him out of the mess he was in.

Charlie let Dennis in on another one of his secrets. His first happy time ended when his father and brother died in a car accident. They were coming home from a ball game. Charlie was happy that the accident happened after the game and not before it. He explained that at least they got to see their team win one last time before they left. He really didn't know if their team won or not, he just assumed that they did.

Charlie lived with his dad, brother and grandfather. They all took very good care of him. After the accident, he only had his grandfather. Spending so much time with him was Charlie's second happy time.

After six years of them being together, his grandpa was also called away by God. That's the way Charlie explained it.

Right after his grandfather's death, Charlie was sent to live in the home. "I just want to be with them again. That is my wish. I tried not good enough. When I leave, it's no tree. I am gonna be with them. Be with them for good." Charlie said, as Dennis noticed a rumbling in the bushes by the road.

Two men started to make their way over to the bench as the orderlies by the main house did as they said they were going to. They turned their heads.

The men made it to their victim and everything went by very fast. It was as if a gust of wind came out of no where and changed many lives forever.

"He's done, he's out. The needle worked just like it was supposed to." One of the men said, as they gathered all of the evidence and loaded up the truck where some other worshipers were waiting.

The orderlies turned back around when everything seemed to be over. All they saw was what appeared to be a happy idiot running over the grounds in a long white robe. "That's just Charlie running off again. Wait until everything is calm and we'll go get him out of his tree once again." One of the orderlies said while laughing.

When everything was quiet again, two of the orderlies headed over to Charlie's tree. As they got closer, they noticed his robe. "See, I told you he would be up in his tree again." One of them said. "Get down here Charlie." The other one said, as he threw a rock up and hit Charlie's robe. As they walked closer, they noticed that Charlie was not in the robe. It was just hanging from a branch.

"That stupid son of a bitch actually ran away this time. I don't believe it." One of them said. Charlie actually out smarted the orderlies this time.

They put out a search party throughout the night to find Charlie. They also told the agents that Dennis was with him when he escaped. The orderlies knew what really happened to Dennis, but they figured it worked out perfect to say it was a break out. The orderlies were happy to get Dennis out of the picture, but if they didn't find Charlie it would bother them because they enjoyed bringing him discomfort.

The search continued for the next couple of days. Nothing was turning up. The news was spread all over the new found religious community that their leader had been sacrificed like he was supposed to be and now it was time to continue worshiping with even more passion for their cause.

It started to get harder and harder for the worshipers to congregate. Law enforcement officials were condemning most of the churches all over the country.

The news of the churches closing made Glenn and Tara and their organization very happy. The news about Dennis being sacrificed for the cause however, brought them a great deal of sorrow.

They didn't believe that Dennis was the organizer of the religion and they suspected something deceitful about Bert when they realized he was against them from the beginning. They just didn't put it together when they should have. Bert almost had Dennis believing that Glenn and Tara were the evil ones, after all of the talking down about them that he did.

The reason St. Barabus didn't seem so evil when Dennis brought Bert to see it was because Bert was able to give Father Servat a warning about the visit.

Glenn and Tara met Rosa, Linda, Amy, Dr. and Mrs. Hynes at a memorial for Dennis. Dr. Hynes informed them of the horrible conference call the night before the sacrifice. He also relayed Dennis' last message to Rosa. She was unable to control her tears and emotions. It was a very sad occasion. They all grieved together.

Up in New England, the excitement continued. There was a small party going on in the house where Amy used to spend most of her time.

Some of the punks she used to hang around with were returning from a graffiti spray painting run. They vandalized many of the fences and garages around the town. When the property owners would go out to paint over their messes, these degenerates would sit in cars parked down the road and shoot the decent citizens in their asses with BB guns. That was just one of their twisted games.

Rayzer and David were also there. Rayzer decided to come out of hiding for the get together. They were talking and laughing about the beating they gave to Dr. Hynes. They thought he was Dennis when they found him in the office, which is why they beat him up.

After an hour or so into the party, a group of men paid them a visit. The men walked from their cars right up to the door and broke it down. They smashed everything in sight with baseball bats. They went on a rampage, cracking the punk's arms, legs and whatever else came at them.

The gang didn't know what hit them. One of them attempted to pull out a gun and take a shot. His hand was quickly smashed by a bat. The gun was the same one that killed Amy's boyfriend, Rick.

The men thought that the gun turning up when the police arrived would make things interesting, so they left it visible. As they were heading out the door, David looked up and asked them where they were from. It was an effort to push the words out from all of the pain he was in.

"Where we come from, friends stick together, we watch each others back's." One man said. "We're from the FARM." Another man added. "What farm?" David grunted. "The Father's Against Rap Music." The man joked, as he laughed and walked out of the door.

The police arrived a few moments after the men left. They brought the whole gang down to the station for a long list of reasons.

The men were Dennis' old friends from the neighborhood. Just like Dennis told Charlie, they would do anything for each other. They thought of it as a good bye present for Dennis. The guys were aware of the trouble that the gang caused for Dennis and they were also given a few tips from David. After all, one of them spent a few days in a cell with David.

G. Novitsky

Chapter Nineteen
"The Truth Always Comes Out"

By this time, I was pretty fed up with everything Bert had done to these people. I also had my own reasons.

My name is Sectat and I knew all of the details that would close this case once and for all. I had been in hiding for quite a while before I decided to take the bold step that I took.

I wrote a letter to Dr. Hynes and Rosa. I asked them to meet me at Dr. Hynes' cabin up in Maine. The letter explained that they would be able to have some sort of satisfaction, although it couldn't bring their friend Dennis back.

Dr. Hynes, Mrs. Hynes, Rosa, Linda and Amy all met me up there early the next Saturday morning. I introduced myself and I told them that before I show them what I brought them up there for, I had one request. The request was for a boat ride once around the area. "Okay kid, this better be worth it though." Dr. Hynes told me.

"Sir, I have been locked up most of my life. When I finally freed myself I had to stay in hiding. I would just like the first of my many trips on your boat to be right now. Would you do that for me?" I asked.

Dr. Hynes wondered where I was going with this request but he was pleased to take the girls and me out for a short trip. It took the nervousness and tensions out of them.

We all had a wonderful time out on the waves. They started to question why I spent most of my life locked up. "That answer and many others will all come in good time. Let's just enjoy the rest of our little cruise, shall we?" I requested.

We only spent an hour or so out on the water. That hour was the most pleasant hour that I ever spent. What a feeling of freedom it was for someone who only knows the scenery of walls.

I laid back on the chase lounge, sipped a cold brew and took in the beautiful sunrays. It was unlike anything I ever dreamed about. The five of them never saw anyone as happy as I was at that moment.

When I was good and ready, we docked the boat and I helped Dr. Hynes tie and pack it in. I asked him if he remembered the construction that was going on by his cabin. "How did you know about that?" He asked.

"I know many interesting things sir. Please call the local police and ask them to pay us a visit." I requested. I could tell that he trusted me. He called the police like I asked without questioning my judgement.

While we waited for the police to come I decided to share a small piece of information with him. I thought about keeping it to myself but someone had to know it. I wanted to share it with Dennis but now, Dr. Hynes would have to be the one. I made him promise that it would stay between him and myself.

I asked him if he knew anything about Amy having any kind of interest in Bert. "Now that you bring it up, the guys did mention something about that once." Dr. Hynes said, as he rubbed his brow. "Do you also recall either of the guys mentioning Bert's brother getting into some trouble while he lived in The States?" I asked, and again Dr. Hynes recalled it.

I explained to him that the trouble he got himself into was getting Rosa pregnant. Bert was actually Amy's uncle. The interest in Bert was based on him having the same eyes as his brother. Neither Rosa nor Amy knew it. Rosa just blocked out the eye thing with her subconscious. The only knowledge of her father's eyes was from the picture Amy kept in her drawer.

Before Dr. Hynes had a chance to comment on the news, four patrol cars pulled up. I brought Dr. Hynes and the police officers over to where the construction took place a while back. The police asked the ladies to keep a safe distance back.

I took a look at the ground and I brushed off an area. I grabbed on to a handle on the ground. I looked up toward the police and Dr. Hynes. "You're gonna love this." I said, as I pulled up on the handle.

The sun light shined in on a stairway. There was sudden movement down at the bottom. The officers pulled out their guns and made their way down the steps, unaware of what they were walking into.

A man approached the stairs, as the officers demanded him to come up and get on the ground. One of the officers cuffed him. It was Carl Morris of Morris Construction Inc.

"Hold on, it gets better." I said, as another man walked toward the stairs and the police demanded him out also. It was panic attack George. They also brought him out with cuffs on.

Some of the police officers stayed up to keep an eye on the prisoners, as the rest accompanied Dr. Hynes, me and the ladies down into the underground mansion-laboratory. I had to assure the police that it was safe for the ladies to follow.

We walked down a hallway and into a small room. The police officers cuffed a few more people on the way. One of them was Mrs. Delancy, Brett's wife.

We entered the small room and just as I anticipated, Bert was standing there with a look of horror on his face. "Officers, please arrest that man!" I said, as they held him to the ground and put the cuffs on him.

The reason the construction didn't seem to go on very long was because it took place underground. Bert picked that spot because he loved the area and he knew Dr. Hynes' cabin was full of supplies in case he ever needed them.

Words could not describe the mixed look of confusion and jubilation on the faces of Dr. Hynes and the ladies. "I only wish Dennis was here for this." He said, as a tear rolled down his cheek.

"I can grant that wish my friend." Dennis said, as he stepped into the room with another police officer. Rosa ran to him and gave him the biggest hug I ever seen one person give to another.

At that moment confusion took on a whole new meaning. Everyone thought that Dennis was dead. Even to my surprise, he was alive and well. "We thought you were gone." Dr. Hynes said, as he grabbed on to Dennis.

"Let's just say I gave a good friend his wish. My pal Charlie is now with his dad, brother and grandfather because he was brave enough to take a needle for me. I guess, charms a third." Dennis explained.

It turned out that Dennis arranged to have Charlie taken away by the worshipers, as he was the one running through the grounds in the white robe. He left the robe in Charlie's tree to throw off the orderlies. Charlie was a big help with the plan.

As for the orderlies, they are now patients in that same insane asylum. The note that Dennis left for Denver was actually directions to accidentally drop that portable stereo in the hot tub while they were taking their nightly soak. The electric shock was not enough to kill them, but it left them in worse shape than Denver or Charlie ever knew. Of course if Denver was tried, he could always plead insanity without a second thought.

When Dennis told that story he called them orglies, like Charlie would have. Dennis also told everyone they could call him Dentist if they wanted to.

After a very joyous reunion, everyone geared their attention toward me. I realized it was time to explain myself.

"Now that I have everyone's attention, here goes. I was born twenty three years ago. I have twelve brothers. Actually, you can call them carbon copies. Let me see if I can get their names right." I went through the list; there was Father Servat, short for Servator, which is Latin for savior. Father Nuntius, meaning messenger. Father Provis, short for provisor, meaning provider. Father Auctoris, meaning creator. Father Disip, short for disipulus, meaning disciple. Father Ducto, short for ductoris, meaning leader or commander. Father Legat, short for legatus, meaning deputy or ambassador. Father Ponde; short for pondere, meaning to spread or to make known. Father Praec, short for praeceptor, meaning teacher or tutor. Father Proteg, short for protegogere, meaning to protect. Father Pater, meaning father or head of the family. And Father Praef, short for praefectus, meaning commander.

I also explained another member of the family named Whitie Exercitatus. Exercitatus is Latin, meaning experienced, trained or disciplined. That was the description of the cloned white tiger.

"You see, I am the only legitimate child of this beast that sits here before you. He studied the Latin language for quite some time. He felt that each of his sons should have a meaningful Latin name. He called himself Domi, which is short for Dominus, meaning Lord. He named me Sectat, short for Sectator, meaning follower. I didn't really appreciate that.

He thought since I was carbon copied so many times it would have drained my intelligence and strength. He felt he could say or do anything he wanted while I was around. I just soaked in all of the information, year after year trapped in that basement, until I was finally able to escape during his move to this place.

He used me to clone all of those others. He set them up in twelve churches all across the United States." I said, as I gave the locations. Rhode Island, South Carolina, Wyoming, Oklahoma, Idaho, Iowa, Utah, South Dakota, Arkansas, Kentucky, Georgia and Tennessee.

The police were about to bring Bert out to the car. The last thing Bert told Dennis was how he was not one to follow rules. After the first sheep was cloned and Whitie was cloned, rule number one became, never to clone a human. He was the first to break that rule. He was able to break it twelve time's twenty-two years before it became a rule.

"One thing before you go Bert. There are no games scheduled for today." Dennis said in a calm relieving voice. Then two officers carried Bert away.

Before Dennis left, I wanted to introduce him to one more person. "Dennis, do you recall my father telling you if you would have solved your first case, this all would have been avoided?" I asked.

He remembered the moment and then I brought him into another room to meet my mother. It was Stephanie. She was the reason Bert and Dennis met. Stephanie was the girl who disappeared twenty four years ago. Bert was hiding her and myself all along in his original laboratory in Connecticut. The building was designed with a laboratory two floors under ground and furnished in a way to raise thirteen children. It was sound proof with a well-hidden entrance. I was conceived the night he first brought Stephanie there.

Mom was wearing her boat and heart charm necklace when I brought Dennis in to meet her.

Bert had the whole upper portion of the Connecticut building taken down recently. He set up the basement the same way as the one we found him in. He had plans to connect all of his underground palaces with the help of Morris Construction Inc. The whole plan had to do with his interest in tunnels connecting land under large spans of water.

Bert pictured tunnels connecting Connecticut to Long Island and in his wildest dreams, the United States to England. He pictured millions of workers in these tunnels as if they were countries of their own. He imagined restaurants, hotels, schools and all kinds of businesses underground connecting countries together. Of course all of the citizens in these underground countries would be worshipers of Domi. That is why he practiced building them under the lake in his back yard.

The funny thing is, no matter how intelligent or educated Bert was, he is now sharing a room with three ex-orderlies in a sanitarium. The day he leaves will be the day he is six feet under in a tunnel like hole dug especially for him.

About the Author

If you thought he couldn't twist your thinking anymore, you're in for a treat. With his unique movie style writing, this Author will take you deep into the pits of his off-centered, bizarre imagination and give new meaning to the question, "What if?"

Printed in the United States
15717LVS00001B/226

9 781410 799296